THE
SHADOW
HEIR

BOOK I OF THE
EVERVEIL CHRONICLLES

STEPHEN M. OVAK

The House of Shadows
Carson City, Nevada

Veritas in Umbra, Fortitudo in Tenebrís.

Truth in Shadow, Strength in Darkness.

For permission requests, contact:
The House of Shadows Publishing
Carson City, Nevada
www.houseofshadowspress.com

Cover Design & Interior Layout:
The House of Shadows Design Collective
Map & Illustrations: Everveil Cartography Guild
(Optional) Add your editor's name here, if desired.

ISBN: 979-8-218-83242-1
Library of Congress Control Number: [Pending]

Printed in the United States of America

EVERVEIL CHRONICLES, BOOK I
THE SHADOW HEIR

TO ALL
THOSE WHO WALK
IN THE SHADOWS
TRYING TO BALANCE
THE LIGHT.

STEPHEN M. OVAK

Author Portrait

AUTHOR'S NOTE

The mythos of *The Shadow Heir* is drawn from a lifetime of stories about the delicate balance between light and shadow. My hope for this series is to carry that torch to a new generation, to illuminate a path between acceptance and defiance—and to remember that even the darkest veil can be parted.

STEPHEN M. OVAK

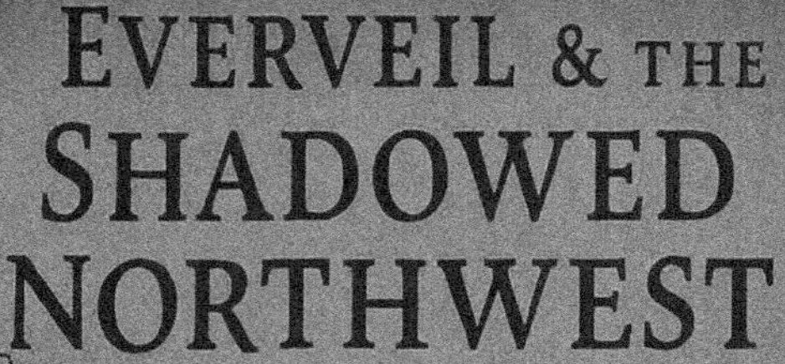

EVERVEIL & THE SHADOWED NORTHWEST
STRAIT OF
DUSK FORU
EVERVEIL INSTITUTE
CALLAM VALLEY
LAKE CRESCENT
LAKE CRESCENT
SULAY MARSH
PACIFICO OCEAN
SHADOW'S HOLLOW
SHADOW'S HOLLOW
SHAMNVDDD
SAMILI
NEHALEM TOWN
MOUNT RAINIER
MT SPIRE

THE EVERVEIL CODEX

(LORE PAGE)

EVERVEIL INSTITUTE

Veritas in Umbra, Fortitudo in Tenebris.

Everveil Institute as school for shadowcraft, orbiting the Pacific Northwest in the States cresting east. Founded in 1867, the Veilguard, the mortal secretkeepers.

THE SEVEN SHADOW HOUSES

The nine shadow clans of antiquity evolved into seven unique houses, representing different aspects of darkness and light.

Truth in Shadow, Strength in Darkness

Great Houses & Their Sigils

House of Shadows

House of Flame

House of Tides

House of Stone

House of Light

House of Storms

House of Mind

"It is said that the Veil is
both a barrier and a bridge—
between the living and the
dead, between the mundane
and the magical, between
man and shadow. This book
tells of sixteen-year-old
Stephen M. Ovak, who once
bore the weight of that bridge."

—EVERVEIL CODEX

PROLOGUE

Whispers Before the Veil

"In the silence between shadow and dawn, the world remembers what it was never meant to know."

Prologue — Whispers Beneath the Veil

The rain fell without mercy over the town of **Duskford**, a place so old it seemed carved from shadow itself. Mist coiled through the crooked streets, swallowing the lanterns and the distant toll of the chapel bell.
At the edge of the forest, where the river met the cliffside, the **Umbral estate** sat in silence — its windows aglow with the faint light of candles that fought against the storm.

Inside, the air was thick with incense and whispers.

Lady **Elara Umbra** lay in her chamber, breath shallow, fingers clawed into the sheets as thunder rolled across the hills. Her husband, **Lord Cael Umbra**, stood by the window — his eyes fixed on the lightning that split the night like a wound.
The servants moved like ghosts, carrying bowls of water and armfuls of white cloth, though none dared speak above a whisper.

When the child's cry finally broke through the storm, the world seemed to hold its breath.

Elara turned her head weakly, tears cutting silver trails across her cheeks.
"Cael," she whispered. "He… he's looking at me."

Cael approached the bedside slowly. The midwife handed him the child — small, pale, and silent now. His eyes were open, wide and gleaming not blue or gray, but **silver**, reflecting the candlelight like mirrors.
For a heartbeat, the thunder stilled.

Elara's voice trembled. "What… what is he seeing?"

Cael didn't answer. He only stared into those eyes — eyes that looked older than the child's heartbeat, older than the house, older than the storm itself.

Then came the whisper.
Soft. Distant. Not human.

"Umbra…"

The torches flickered.
The silver in the child's gaze deepened, and for an instant, the shadows along the wall seemed to bend toward him — drawn, not by light, but by blood.

Elara gasped and reached out. "Cael, do you hear it?"

He nodded once, though his throat had gone dry.
"I do. The Veil… it's watching."

A sound came then — not thunder, but something beneath it.
A low hum that seemed to rise from the earth itself, reverberating through the stone floors of the manor.
The midwife dropped her bowl and fled the room. Only Cael and Elara remained, and the child between them.

Elara reached for her son again, pressing her lips to his forehead. Her voice broke as she whispered, "Stephen… my little shadow."

The moment she spoke his name, the candles went out.

The room was swallowed by darkness.
Then — just as swiftly — every candle reignited, each flame burning with a faint silver hue instead of gold.

Cael looked down. The child was calm now, his small hand reaching upward, fingers brushing the air as though tracing

unseen shapes.
A mark shimmered briefly upon his wrist — a crescent eclipsed by a shadow.

The mark of the **Umbra line**.

Outside, the rain slowed to a whisper, and the wind seemed to sigh in reverence.
Somewhere deep in the woods, a raven cried — once, twice — before silence reclaimed the night.

Elara fell asleep then, her hand resting upon her son's chest. Cael turned toward the window, watching as the storm retreated beyond the horizon. "You'll bear more than any child should," he murmured. "But you are ours — and you will carry our truth."

The silver light dimmed. The child's eyes closed.

And for the first time since the founding of the Umbra line, the shadows around the house **bowed** — not to darkness, but to the one born to walk between it and the light.

Chapter I — The Boy and the Shadow

The rain had not stopped for three days.
In Duskford, storms always lingered longer when the old
powers stirred.

Inside the Umbra estate, firelight wavered across black oak
and iron fixtures, throwing restless shapes along the walls. The
hearth glowed low, the air rich with pine resin and candle
smoke. The night felt heavy — watchful.

It was **Stephen Erebus Umbra's fifteenth birthday.**

His parents had chosen a quiet celebration. The table was set
with silver, a single cake, and a pot of tea that had long gone
cold. No guests, no laughter — only the three of them and the
distant sound of rain against glass.

At the head of the table sat **Cael Umbra**, tall and sharp-
featured, his dark coat trimmed in silver thread. Across from
him, **Elara Umbra** moved with quiet grace, her hands folded,
her gaze soft but shadowed. Between them sat Stephen, who
had the feeling that this wasn't just a birthday — it was a
reckoning.

When the last of the candles guttered low, Cael rose without a
word and crossed to the cabinet by the window. From it, he
drew a long, narrow object wrapped in black silk.

He laid it on the table. The room seemed to breathe in.

Elara touched her son's arm gently. "Before you open it," she
said softly, "you must understand — this is not a gift. It's an
inheritance."

Cael unwrapped the silk.

A **book** lay beneath — old, bound in dark hide that shimmered faintly as though alive. Silver thread stitched its edges into a crescent devoured by shadow: the **Umbra family crest.**

Stephen leaned closer. "That's the one from your study," he said, his voice a whisper. "The one I'm not supposed to touch."

Cael's eyes glinted faintly in the firelight. "And tonight, you'll learn why."

Elara's smile was warm but weary. "You've always felt it, haven't you? The hum in the air when you're afraid. The way the dark listens when you speak."

Stephen's breath caught. "You know about that?"

"We've always known," she said. "You were born of two lines — Umbra and Nox. The Walkers of Shadow and the Binders of Night. When those bloods meet, the Veil listens."

Cael rested his hands upon the book. "It's your birthright, Stephen. But it's also your burden. You carry both the light and the dark within you — the harmony of what the world once feared to remember."

He opened the book.

Instantly, the candles bent inward. The hearth crackled once, and the air filled with a low hum that vibrated through the floor. Symbols surfaced on the page, glowing silver like veins of moonlight.

Elara whispered, *"Veritas in Umbra, Fortitudo in Tenebris."*
Her voice trembled with reverence.
"Truth in Shadow. Strength in Darkness."

The family creed.

Stephen reached toward the page. The moment his fingers
brushed the surface, light burst from the text — crawling up
his arm, etching a mark across his wrist: a crescent moon
consumed by shadow.

The Umbra sigil.

When the glow faded, the storm outside eased into mist. For a
heartbeat, all was still.

Cael spoke softly. "You're bound now. The Veil has seen
you."

Stephen looked down at the mark. "What does it want from
me?"

His father's tone darkened. "It wants to test you. To teach you.
You'll leave for **Everveil Institute** when the next full moon
rises."

Stephen's pulse quickened. "Leave? Where?"

Elara stepped closer, her voice low and steady. "To the north,
beyond the Cascades. A school built where the Veil is
thinnest. It's where those born with shadow in their blood go
to learn control. Your father studied there, long ago."

Cael gave a single nod. "When the time comes, a carriage will
arrive at dusk, drawn by black steeds. You'll recognize it by
our sigil. You'll travel through the misted pass. Three days'
journey."

Stephen's eyes darted between them. "And if I don't?"

Cael's voice left no room for doubt. "Then the Veil will come for you."

The words hung in the air like prophecy.

Elara touched his shoulder. "You have two weeks, my son. Two weeks to prepare. Use them well."

That night, Stephen couldn't sleep. The Umbra book lay open on his desk, whispering softly in a tongue he didn't yet know. Outside, the forest shimmered under a thin veil of fog.

And somewhere beyond the trees, the shadows shifted — slow, deliberate, listening.

He whispered, "I can hear you."

And from the dark, something answered.

Then it's time you remembered who you are

Chapter II — The Whispering Veil

The days after Stephen's fifteenth birthday passed like falling embers—bright for a moment, then lost to the dark.
He rose before dawn each morning, watching the fog drift from the Duskford woods beyond the Umbra estate. The mist never truly cleared. It clung to the earth as though reluctant to leave, whispering secrets he couldn't quite hear.

His father, **Cael Umbra**, had become quieter since the awakening. He still spoke to Stephen, but every conversation carried the weight of unspoken things—warnings that didn't yet have words.
His mother, **Elara**, on the other hand, seemed both nearer and farther at once. She would touch his shoulder when she passed, trace the mark on his wrist with a thoughtful expression, and say softly, "The Veil watches through every shadow."

Stephen had begun to believe her.

The Dreams

They started two nights after his marking.
He dreamt of corridors that stretched forever, lined with mirrors that didn't reflect him. Each pane shimmered faintly, showing flickers of movement—like someone walking behind the glass.
Each night, the dream grew clearer. The mirrors began to hum, and when he tried to touch one, a voice would whisper:

"The path opens when the moon divides."

He would wake gasping, the mark on his wrist burning faintly.
Every morning, the same mist pressed against his window,

curling into faint shapes like reaching hands before vanishing
with the dawn.

By the fourth night, he no longer told his parents.
Not because he didn't trust them—but because deep down, he
knew the dreams weren't warnings.
They were invitations.

The Book and the Shadow

The Umbra tome had changed, too.
Its cover now pulsed faintly when he drew near, the silver
threads glimmering with a heartbeat that didn't belong to the
house.
On the seventh night, he found new writing on its first page—
thin, silvery letters scrawled in a hand he didn't recognize.

To walk the shadow, one must first be seen by it.

He traced the words, and the candles in his room dimmed.
The shadows along the wall deepened, curling into the faint
outline of a figure—vague, shifting, faceless.

Stephen froze. "Who are you?"

The figure tilted its head. Its voice came like breath through
glass.

A reflection.
A guide.
A promise.

The shape dissolved before he could answer, leaving only the
faint scent of cold air and the rustle of unseen wings.

The Lesson of Silence

The next morning, Cael called him to the family study. Books lay stacked in uneven towers, and the window drapes were drawn against the sun.

"Your mother tells me the shadows have started to speak," Cael said without preamble.

Stephen hesitated. "You can tell?"

Cael's smile was grim. "When the Veil marks one of our blood, the air itself begins to change. Doors open that should stay closed. That's why you must learn restraint."

He stepped closer, placing a small black stone on the table between them. Its surface was smooth, etched with faint silver veins.

"This is an anchor," Cael said. "When the shadows reach for you, place it on your palm and breathe. It binds your thoughts to the light—keeps the dark from listening too deeply."

Stephen took it carefully. "What happens if I don't?"

His father's eyes darkened. "Then the Veil stops whispering and starts answering."

Departure Approaches

Two weeks passed quickly.

The morning of the full moon dawned with crimson light over Duskford. The air was heavy, still, as if the world itself held its breath.

Elara packed his satchel in silence: ink, parchment, the anchor stone, and a small crest of silver shaped like a crescent moon. When she clasped it to his cloak, she whispered, "No matter what you see beyond those mountains, remember who you are. You are not the shadow. You are what stands between it and the world."

Stephen nodded, unable to speak.

By dusk, thunder rolled across the valley.
Through the fog came the sound of hooves—slow, deliberate, echoing. A carriage emerged from the mist, drawn by two black steeds whose eyes glowed faintly silver. The driver wore no face—only a dark hood and gloves.

Cael placed a hand on his son's shoulder. "You'll reach Everveil by dawn. Don't speak to the driver. Don't look out the window once you cross the first bridge."

Elara embraced him tightly. "The Veil doesn't test what's weak, Stephen. It tests what's worthy."

He climbed aboard. The door shut behind him with a whisper that wasn't sound. As the carriage began to move, he glanced back—his parents stood framed in the doorway, two silhouettes burning like lanterns in the fog.

When the road turned north, the mist thickened until the world beyond the glass vanished.

And somewhere in the endless dark ahead, faint lights flickered—towers rising through the mountain fog.

Everveil awaited.

Chapter III — The Road to Everveil

(Canon-Perfect Revision)

The journey north began in silence.
The road wound through forests so dense the moonlight could barely slip between the branches. Mist hung over everything—curling around the wheels of the black carriage, swallowing the world beyond its glass.

Stephen sat alone inside, the anchor stone in his hand. It pulsed faintly against his palm, steady as a heartbeat.
The Umbra crest sewn into his cloak shimmered when the moonlight found it—a half-wolf silhouette eclipsing a crescent moon.

Outside, the horses made no sound. The driver's hooded figure didn't move. Even the trees seemed to lean away from the road as if refusing to witness who passed through.

The air grew colder. And though no words were spoken, Stephen could feel something *watching*.

The Voice in the Fog

It came softly, threading through the mist like the breath of a dying flame.

"Are you the Umbra heir?"

He stiffened. His father's warning echoed in his mind.
Don't speak. Don't answer anything that calls your name on the road.

He said nothing.

The voice chuckled. "Silence is wise. The shadows remember those who listen."

A cold pressure pressed against the carriage wall, like a hand without form.
The glass frosted over for a moment—and when it cleared, his reflection was gone.

He shut his eyes, clutching the anchor stone until the heat returned to his fingers.

When he opened them again, the voice—and the presence— were gone.

The Gate of Everveil

He awoke to the soft creak of the carriage stopping. Dawn burned faintly behind the mountains, painting the fog with silver light.

Before him rose the gates of **Everveil Institute**—massive and wrought of black iron, engraved with glowing sigils that pulsed like veins. The center bore seven emblems, each for a House of Shadowcraft.

At the heart of them all gleamed the crescent and wolf of the **House of Shadows**.

The door opened on its own. The fog reached inside as if to welcome him.

Stephen stepped down, boots sinking into wet stone, and felt an almost magnetic pull—an energy humming beneath his skin. The mountain itself seemed alive.

The Keeper of the Gate

"Stephen Umbra," said a voice behind him.

He turned.
A tall woman stood at the threshold, wrapped in a cloak of gray silk embroidered with silver thread. Her eyes glowed faintly violet in the mist.

"I am **Headmistress Veyra Thorne**, Keeper of the Veil," she said.
"You've arrived later than most."

"I didn't realize there was a schedule," Stephen said quietly.

"There always is," she replied. "Everveil waits for no one—but sometimes, it watches."

She raised a hand, and the runes along the gate flickered to life. "Beyond these doors lies the path to the seven Houses. Each will test what you bring and what you lack. You'll find the orientation hall at the top of the lantern path. And one more thing…"

Her tone softened. "Don't step beyond the lantern light. The shadows here are… older than the walls."

She turned to leave, fading into mist as though she had never existed.

The Path of Lanterns

Stephen followed the winding trail up the mountainside. Lanterns hung from iron posts along the path, glowing faintly blue. Each time he passed one, the light brightened—then dimmed again behind him, like a heartbeat echoing in the fog.

He saw other students on the trail ahead—no familiars yet, only silhouettes in dark cloaks carrying suitcases and books. Some whispered to one another, but most kept their eyes on the ground.

At one turn, Stephen glanced back.
The valley below was gone. Only mist remained, shifting and alive, hiding everything he had ever known.

The First Sight of Everveil

When he reached the ridge, the full scope of the Institute revealed itself.

A vast fortress rose from the mountainside—towers of obsidian stone veined with faint silver light. Bridges arched between them high above the ground, lined with blue lanterns that pulsed like stars.

In the courtyard below, instructors moved like wraiths, their robes whispering against the marble. Students gathered in silence, their expressions a mix of awe and fear.

And above it all, carved into the mountainside itself, a great sigil glowed faintly—half wolf, half moon—watching.

Stephen stood there, the wind curling through his hair, and understood what his mother meant when she said: *"The Veil watches through every shadow."*

Everveil was alive.
And it had been waiting for him.

Chapter IV — The Sorting of Shadows

The Great Hall of Everveil was carved from living stone —
black marble shot through with veins of starlight. The air
shimmered with silver embers that drifted like falling ash.
Long tables of obsidian lined the room, but no one sat. The
new students stood in silence beneath the towering vaulted
ceiling, staring upward at the illusion of a night sky that
pulsed faintly with its own heartbeat.

The seven banners of the Houses hung above the dais, each
marked by its sigil:

- **House of Shadows** — a crescent moon eclipsed by a
  wolf's head.
- **House of Flame** — a phoenix rising through smoke.
- **House of Stone** — a mountain split by a single silver
  line.
- **House of Tides** — a wave curling into a spiral over an
  eye.
- **House of Storms** — a lightning bolt coiled within a
  ring of mist.
- **House of Light** — a radiant sun encircled by broken
  chains.
- **House of Mind** — a silver eye framed by three runic
  lines.

Each banner glowed softly, waiting.

At the center of the dais, Headmistress **Veyra Thorne** raised
her staff — a length of blackened yew topped with a shard of
crystal that pulsed with a heartbeat of its own. Her silver hair
framed her face like a crown of light and shadow.

"Welcome to Everveil," she said, her voice both warm and
dreadful. "Here, the Veil watches. The power that hides
between worlds does not *ask* who you are — it *shows* you.

When you stand in the circle, the shadows will find your truth."

The Shadowcall Begins

At her signal, the floor at the hall's center began to shift. Stone spiraled inward, etching glowing runes in a perfect circle. From its depths, black mist rose — thin at first, then thicker, until it stood like smoke given life. The students instinctively stepped back.

Veyra's voice echoed. "Step forward when your name is called. The Veil will test your heart. Do not fight it."

The first student stepped forward, trembling. The shadows parted slightly as they entered the ring, curling around their ankles like fog. Then the mist rose, swift as a storm, enveloping them entirely.

For a moment, there was only darkness. Then — **fire.**
A pillar of orange light burst upward, and the phoenix banner flared to life. The student gasped as embers rained down, vanishing before they touched the ground.

"House of Flame!" Veyra declared.

The hall erupted in applause, half awe, half fear.

One by one, students stepped into the circle. The shadows shifted — turning to waves, to lightning, to stone, each form born from the essence of the chosen House. No two displays were the same; the Veil shaped itself to the soul it touched.

Stephen's Turn

When Veyra finally spoke his name — *"Stephen Erebus Umbra."* — the air itself seemed to still.

He stepped forward slowly. The circle pulsed in anticipation. The moment his foot crossed the threshold, the mist reacted violently, coiling around him like a living storm. Gasps echoed through the hall. The shadows climbed his body, swirling around his arms and throat, until he was completely engulfed.

For an instant, he felt nothing — then *everything*.
A thousand whispers pressed against his skull, speaking his name in voices that weren't voices at all. He saw flashes — a silver wolf beneath a dying moon, a blade made of living night, a gate standing open between worlds.

Then the darkness exploded.

The shadows burst upward in a spiraling column, wrapping the hall in an eclipse. Candles guttered out. The banners flared violently, their light dimming one by one until only one remained — the **House of Shadows**.

The air was thick and electric. The shadows coalesced into a massive, translucent wolf made entirely of mist and starlight. It stood behind Stephen, lowering its head as if in recognition.

Veyra lowered her staff slowly, her expression unreadable. "The House of Shadows claims its heir."

The wolf dissolved into silver smoke that sank into Stephen's chest, leaving behind a faint mark — a crescent etched in light just above his heart.

The hall erupted in murmurs. Some bowed their heads. Others stepped back, wary. The Shadows had chosen heirs before — but never with such violence, such spectacle.

The House of Shadows

When the ceremony ended, the new students followed their House guides through the winding corridors. Stephen's group descended a spiral stair into a colder, quieter part of the fortress. Torches burned blue here, their flames whispering faintly as if speaking in a forgotten tongue.

At the end of the hall stood a door of black iron, carved with the sigil of the crescent wolf. It opened on its own as they approached.

Inside, a tall man waited — **Master Kaelith Dorn**, Shadowwarden of the House. His pale eyes glimmered faintly in the dark.

"Welcome," he said softly. "Here you will learn not to fear the dark… but to *become* it."

His gaze settled on Stephen. "Umbra. The blood returns. I suppose the Veil has decided to stir old ghosts."

Stephen said nothing. He could still feel the mark on his chest burning faintly.

That night, when the others slept, he woke to whispers again — faint, beckoning.
Find the Door, Heir of Umbra. The Veil remembers you.

He looked toward the shadows — and thought, for the briefest second, that they looked back.

Chapter V — The Boy in the Quiet Hall

The mountain slept, but Everveil did not.
Through the stone corridors of the House of Shadows, the torches burned in silence — pale blue flames that moved like breath, faintly reacting to every heartbeat that passed.

Stephen Umbra walked alone. He should have been in his dorm by now, but rest had been impossible since the Shadowcall. His thoughts looped endlessly: the rising veil, the whisper that had spoken his name, and the wolf-shape in the smoke that had looked straight through him.

He paused at a turning. The walls here shimmered faintly, threaded with silver veins that pulsed like arteries of the mountain itself.

Then a voice spoke from the dark.
"You're walking the shifting corridors. Either you're brave… or lost."

Stephen turned.
A boy about his age stood half in shadow, half in torchlight — sharp-featured, dark-haired, with an expression of curious detachment. His uniform was worn in the way that said he'd been here longer.

"I'm guessing you're the first-year everyone's whispering about," the boy said. "Stephen Umbra."

Stephen tensed. "Who are you?"

"Kael Thane," he replied, stepping into the light. "Second-year. You can relax — I'm not going to hex you."

Stephen blinked. "Didn't think you were."

"Good," Kael said. "Because you wouldn't block it anyway."

The Library of Veils

Kael motioned down a side passage. "Come on. You're already breaking curfew. Might as well see something worth getting caught for."

He led Stephen through a series of spiraling staircases that seemed to breathe. Eventually, they stopped before a tall iron door. Symbols pulsed faintly along its frame — the same sigils carved into the Great Hall's ring.

Kael pressed his hand to the surface. The metal rippled like liquid shadow and folded open.

"The Library of Veils," he said. "Technically off-limits. But I figured you'd want to see it before they drown you in lectures."

The chamber beyond seemed endless. Shelves curved into impossible arches, books humming softly with breath-like motion. Lanterns floated in slow orbits, casting moving patterns across the walls. The air smelled of dust, ozone, and ink — old, heavy, alive.

Stephen whispered, "It's beautiful."

Kael's tone softened. "It's dangerous. Every book here remembers something the world was supposed to forget."

Reflections

They sat at one of the long tables. For a while, neither spoke. The silence wasn't uncomfortable — just dense, like the air before a storm.

Kael finally said, "Just had a birthday, didn't you?"
Stephen looked up. "Two days ago."
Kael nodded, the faintest smile tugging at his mouth. "That explains the stir in the halls. Things tend to wake up around birthdays — especially the kind that matter."

Stephen frowned. "You mean because of my name?"

"I mean because of your bloodline," Kael said. "Umbra isn't a quiet name. The walls remember it."

He leaned back in his chair, studying him. "You'll learn this soon enough — the Veil doesn't just watch. It waits. Sometimes for years."

Stephen hesitated. "You sound like someone who's seen it waiting."

"I have," Kael said quietly. "On my birthday, last year. October thirty-first. The Night of Veils. The sky split open, and the Headmaster called it a coincidence."

"Was it?"

Kael's eyes glimmered faintly in the dim light. "There are no coincidences here. Only warnings we don't want to read."

The Whisper

One of the lanterns above them flickered, dimming until the air felt cold.
A faint murmur slid through the space, soft as a sigh.

"Two bound by shadow. One to remember. One to awaken."

The whisper faded, and the light steadied.

Stephen swallowed. "What was that?"
Kael didn't answer at first. His eyes stayed on the ceiling, thoughtful, not frightened.
"That's the mountain," he said finally. "Or maybe the Veil. Hard to tell. Sometimes it talks."

"Does it always sound so—"
"Old?" Kael finished. "Yeah. Everything down here is old. We're just… borrowed time."

Stephen looked at him. "You're not afraid."
Kael met his gaze, calm and unreadable. "I was. First year. You stop being afraid once you realize fear's the thing it listens for."

They left the Library in silence.
Behind them, one lantern flared briefly, casting twin shadows on the far wall — a flicker of two figures walking side by side into the dark.

Outside, the wind rose against the mountain, and somewhere below, the Veil stirred — faintly aware that two pieces of something ancient had finally found each other again.

Chapter VI — Whispers Beneath the Stone

Morning light never touched the House of Shadows.
Instead, its halls woke to the slow dim glow of the rune-lamps,
kindled one by one by unseen hands. The air smelled faintly of
chalk and incense, a blend of ritual and stone.

Stephen Umbra rose with the rest of the first-years, the distant
chime of bells echoing through the dormitory vaults. He had
barely slept — not after the whispers in the library. His
dreams had been thick with shadow, filled with echoing voices
he could not remember upon waking.

Across the room, Kael Thane leaned against a pillar, watching
the new students stumble from their bunks with the weary
amusement of someone who had done this before.

"You'll get used to the bells," Kael said. "Eventually, you
won't even hear them."

Stephen smirked faintly. "That sounds more like death than
adjustment."
"Close enough," Kael said, straightening his coat. "Come on.
You don't want to be late for initiation lectures. They start
with the polite ones before the real ones begin."

The Morning Assembly

The House gathered in the atrium — a vast, circular chamber
lined with black marble pillars and carved banners of onyx
thread. At its center hung the **Crest of Shadows**: a silver wolf
eclipsed by a crescent moon, suspended in air by unseen
runes.

Head of House, **Magister Alaric Vale**, stood before them. His voice carried with the measured calm of a storm that knew exactly when to strike.

"Shadow is not absence," Alaric began. "It is memory. A record of all light that has passed. Here, you will learn not to flee from darkness — but to read it."

Stephen felt the words sink deep into him, resonating like a bell through bone. Around him, the students stood in silence, the weight of initiation already pressing down.

Kael glanced his way. "He says that same speech every year," he whispered. "Still gives me chills."

Stephen whispered back, "Maybe that's the point."

First Lessons

Their first class was **Umbral Theory**, held in a low, echoing hall whose walls were covered in spectral diagrams. The instructor, **Professor Selene Corren**, was young by Everveil's standards — sharp-eyed, her robes lined with silver glyphs that shimmered faintly when she moved.

"Shadowcraft is not conjuration," she said. "It is resonance. Every shadow has a heart, every heart has a reflection. What we call power is only understanding what already exists."

She drew a thin line of black light through the air, shaping it into a sigil.
"Your first task," she said, "is not to make the shadow obey — but to make it listen."

Stephen tried. For nearly an hour, his shadow barely stirred. Then, during a moment of frustration, the ink bottle on his desk trembled, and the shadow beneath his hand *shifted*.

It wasn't obedience — it was attention. The shadow looked back.

Professor Corren's eyes flicked toward him, her expression unreadable. "Good," she said softly. "The Veil remembers its own."

Whispers Between Lessons

By afternoon, the school was alive.
Students crossed the bridges between towers, shadows trailing like smoke. From the House of Flame came bursts of firelight; from the House of Mind, soft murmurs like chanting. Bells tolled faintly from distant towers — Everveil's strange heartbeat.

Kael fell into step beside Stephen as they made their way toward the dining hall. "So, how does it feel?"

Stephen hesitated. "Like the mountain's watching me."

Kael grinned. "It is. It watches everyone. You'll stop noticing after a few years."

They passed a group of third-years, their uniforms marked with glowing sigils. One whispered something that made the others laugh — but Stephen caught a word: *Umbra*.

He frowned. "They know my name."
"They know your bloodline," Kael corrected. "There's a difference."

Stephen looked away. "Feels like the same thing."
Kael didn't answer. He just said, "You'll understand soon
enough. The mountain doesn't forget its heirs."

Nightfall

When night returned, Stephen sat at his desk by the window,
the moon faint behind the mist. His journal lay open, the ink
glimmering faintly in the low light.

The shadows don't just move here. They listen.
Sometimes I think they're trying to remember something —
through me.

From the corridor outside came a soft sound — like stone
shifting. He turned toward the door. Nothing.
Then a faint, almost imperceptible whisper:

"Awaken, heir of Umbra."

The candle flickered out.

Chapter VII — The Hidden Pulse

The mornings in Everveil had a way of tricking the mind. Even after a week, Stephen Umbra couldn't tell if it was the sunlight breaking through the fog or the mountain's own shadow lifting for a while. The air always held a soft hum — not quite sound, not quite silence — like the heartbeat of something sleeping just below.

He woke before the bells again, breath fogging the air. The dormitory windows were rimmed with frost, their panes whispering as though the glass itself dreamed.

He rubbed his temples and sat up, squinting into the dim light that bled through the curtains. For a moment, he thought he saw movement in the corner — his own shadow, stretching slightly before settling back into place.

"Not again," he muttered.
But even as he said it, the shadow's edges curled like smoke.

Then the bell rang — one, two, three — and the darkness retreated, as if chased back into the walls.

The Hall of Veils

By mid-morning, the students of the House of Shadows assembled in the lower hall — a place older than most of the towers above. The stones here were black, veined with silver that pulsed faintly under the torchlight.

Professor Selene Corren stood at the front, her robe of deep gray edged in soft light, each thread shimmering like frost on steel. Her silver hair was bound in a long braid, her expression unreadable as she spoke.

"These halls," she began, voice echoing, "were not *built* by the founders of Everveil. They were *claimed*."

Her hand brushed the nearest wall. The surface responded with a low hum, rippling faintly like disturbed water.

"They say the Hall of Veils was carved from the bones of an older temple — one devoted not to the gods, but to the *space between them.* To the silence that breathes between worlds."

Stephen felt the air around him grow heavier. His eyes drifted toward one of the tall, narrow mirrors lining the wall. It reflected light, but not perfectly. His reflection seemed slightly… delayed, like a heartbeat half a moment behind.

When he blinked, the reflection didn't.

Kael Thane leaned closer, his voice low. "Don't stare too long. The Veil watches back."

Stephen turned away, his pulse hammering. "You're joking."
"Wish I was," Kael said, his lips twitching in a humorless smirk.

Professor Corren's voice carried on, steady as ever. "The Veil remembers everything that passes through it — faces, voices, even lies. And sometimes, it reflects what we've forgotten."

The Library of Whispers

That night, the air was too thick for sleep.
Stephen sat at his desk, staring at the crescent mark carved faintly into the spine of his student ledger. It seemed to shimmer under moonlight, though he knew it shouldn't.

Somewhere below the dorms, a low vibration rolled through the foundation — too steady to be wind, too deep to be footsteps.

He threw on his cloak and stepped out.

The corridors of the House of Shadows were never truly dark; faint wisps of light drifted along the arches, tracing runes too ancient for modern tongues. The sound led him downward — toward the library vaults.

He wasn't alone. Kael sat by one of the great tables, a single lantern casting gold across his pale hair and sharp features. Before him lay an enormous tome bound in black leather and marked with silver seals.

"You heard it too," Stephen said.

Kael looked up. "Heard it? I felt it. Like the mountain's breathing again."
"What is it?"
Kael shrugged. "Some say the Veil itself hums when it's weak. Others say… it hums when something's trying to push through."

He turned the page, and the candle flickered violently. The ink on the parchment rippled as if alive, forming symbols neither of them had seen before.

A sigil emerged — a **crescent surrounded by seven orbs**, connected by fine lines like veins of light.

Beneath it, in letters scorched faintly into the paper, was a single phrase:

When the Veil breathes, the Door stirs.

Kael whispered, "What door?"

Stephen didn't answer. The hum was louder now — closer.

The Subterranean Stair

The next night, it came again. Stronger.
The ink in their bottles rippled. Books vibrated on their
shelves.

Kael was already at Stephen's door when he opened it. "You
feel that?"
Stephen nodded. "It's coming from below."
"Then we follow it."

They slipped through the hall, their footsteps muffled by
enchanted carpets, the only sound the low rhythmic thrum that
pulsed through the stone.

Down they went — past the study halls, past the sealed
archives. The air grew colder, the lamps dimmer. The sound
deepened until they could feel it in their ribs.

At last they reached a corridor they had never seen before — a
narrow passage ending in a wall carved with hundreds of
runes. Most were faint, but one burned faintly with blue light:
the crescent and seven dots.

Stephen raised his hand. The sigil *reacted.*

Stone flowed like smoke, curling away from his touch,
revealing a hidden archway. Beyond it, a staircase spiraled
down into blackness.

Kael whispered, "I don't think we're supposed to be here."
Stephen took a breath. "Neither do I."
Then he stepped forward.

The Door That Breathes

The stair opened into a cavern vast enough to swallow the castle above. The walls pulsed faintly, alive with veins of silver that beat like a heart beneath stone.

And there, at the far end, stood the Door.
It was circular, seamless, carved from a single piece of obsidian so polished it reflected their torchlight like liquid.

Every few seconds, its surface rippled. Like a lung drawing breath.

Kael's voice was barely a whisper. "Is it… alive?"
Stephen didn't answer. Something about it felt *familiar* — like the pulse he'd felt every morning since arriving.

He stepped closer, his shadow stretching unnaturally ahead of him. The closer he came, the brighter the sigil on the door burned — the same crescent and seven lights, now glowing silver-blue.

When he reached out, the light surged.
The air shattered into mist and wind. Kael shouted, but the sound drowned beneath the roar.

Stephen's hand touched the surface — and the world collapsed into shadow.

When he awoke, the dormitory bells were tolling dawn.
Kael lay beside him, pale and breathing shallowly. The mark
on Stephen's palm glowed faintly, pulsing with the same
rhythm as the Door.

He turned it over, heart pounding.
The crescent-and-seven was burned into his flesh.

And when the bells stopped ringing, the hum beneath the
mountain did not.

Chapter VIII — The Echo in the Veil

The week after the discovery felt different.
The air within Everveil had always hummed faintly, but now the vibration carried through everything — the walls, the windows, even the silver cutlery in the dining hall. Most students brushed it off as mountain weather. But Stephen and Kael knew better. They could feel it — a pulse in rhythm with the mark now carved into Stephen's hand.

He'd tried covering it with gloves, even wrapping it in bandages, but the light bled through at night — faint silver threads that danced beneath his skin, pulsing to an unseen heartbeat.

Kael pretended not to notice, though his eyes always lingered longer than they should.

Whispers in the Reflection

The Hall of Mirrors had been closed for years — "unstable enchantments," the instructors said. Which, at Everveil, meant *interesting*.

Kael found it first. "The southern wing's open again," he whispered over breakfast, sliding a folded note toward Stephen. "Corren's class got moved there this afternoon."

Stephen frowned. "You're sure?"
Kael grinned. "I may have helped it open."

By the time they arrived, the hall was colder than it should have been. The air smelled of iron and rain. Silver torches lined the walls, their flames burning in reverse — black fire with white smoke.

Professor Corren stood before the mirrors, her expression sharp but unreadable. "These were once used to test resonance between a student's essence and the Veil's current. We abandoned them when they began showing *too much.*"

Stephen's chest tightened. The nearest mirror shimmered, and his reflection leaned closer — smiling faintly even though he wasn't.

Corren's voice softened. "Control is not about suppression, Umbra. It's about acknowledgment. Shadows are mirrors of truth, not of fear."

The reflection's smile vanished. Then, impossibly, it *spoke.* "You touched the Door."

Stephen stumbled backward.
Corren's head snapped up. "What did you say?"
But the mirror had gone still. Only Kael had heard it too — his face pale.

The Raven and the Wolf

That night, thunder rolled across the Cascades.
The storm painted the sky in silver veins, and the mountain wind screamed through the towers like an instrument of bone.

Stephen couldn't sleep. The mark on his hand burned faintly — a steady throb that matched the rhythm of the rain.

He walked out to the courtyard, where the storm-wet stones glimmered like obsidian. Kael found him there, drenched, hood drawn low.

"You heard it, didn't you?" Kael asked.
Stephen nodded. "It knew about the Door. How?"
"Maybe it didn't. Maybe it *was* the Door."

The wind shifted.
A low, haunting caw echoed through the night — a raven's call, but stretched too long, almost human. Both boys turned toward the far parapet, where a single raven sat, wings slicked with rain, eyes glowing faintly silver.

It tilted its head. Then it vanished into smoke.

The mark on Stephen's hand pulsed once — hard enough to make him stagger.
Kael caught his arm. "It's calling to you."

Stephen swallowed. "Then maybe we should stop answering."

The Forbidden Archives

The next morning, the two slipped into the western wing. It wasn't on the student maps — likely because most of it had been sealed since before either of them were born.

The walls here were covered in relief carvings: figures kneeling before a great, circular door carved into a mountain's heart. Above it, the same sigil — the crescent and seven lights — and the old Everveil motto:

Veritas in Umbra. Fortitudo in Tenebris.
Truth in Shadow. Strength in Darkness.

Kael traced the inscription. "You think the school was built around it?"
Stephen nodded. "Not around it. *Because of it.*"

They reached the final chamber — round, domed, and lined with iron shelves. Parchments hung in the air like suspended smoke, pages whispering softly as if breathing.

In the center stood a pedestal — atop it, a fragment of black glass. Its surface pulsed faintly with that same rhythm Stephen now felt in his bones.

He reached for it, but Kael grabbed his wrist. "Last time you touched something that glowed, you woke up a day later."
"I have to know what it is."

The light flared. A shockwave of sound tore through the room — every hanging parchment fluttering violently. The air bent, colors rippling like liquid shadow.

And then they heard it again: the *voice*.

"The mark awakens the bond.
The Door remembers its heirs."

Kael shouted, "Who's there?"
But the light had already faded. The fragment lay still again, dull and lifeless.

Echoes in the Veil

By the time they escaped the Archives, dawn was breaking. The mountain fog glowed faint silver, and the world felt… thinner.

Kael broke the silence first. "You're sure it said 'heirs'? Not 'error'?"
Stephen's expression was grave. "Heirs. Like descendants."
"Of what?"

Stephen looked back toward the school towers, half-shrouded in mist. "I think Everveil remembers more than people realize."

The wind howled through the peaks, carrying faint whispers that sounded almost like laughter.
And beneath it all — the mountain's heartbeat continued, slow and relentless.

Chapter IX — The Night of Falling Mirrors

The rain had not stopped for two days.

It came down in silver sheets that blurred the world beyond
Everveil's windows, washing the courtyard clean of color and
swallowing the mountain paths in fog. Students muttered
about storms and sleepless nights.
But in the House of Shadows, every torch burned lower.

Stephen hadn't been the same since the Archives. He kept
catching glimpses of movement in polished surfaces — not
reflections, but shadows of himself that lingered too long.
Kael noticed first.

"You've been twitching every time you walk past glass," Kael
said, throwing a small pebble at him across the dorm table.
Stephen caught it without looking up. "Because it twitches
back."

The Mirror Fractures

That night, the school bell tolled — a sound deep and
sonorous, shaking the foundations of the tower.
It was nearly midnight. No bells should have been ringing.

Stephen and Kael were already awake. They stepped into the
corridor as other students stirred, whispering. The torches
along the walls flickered, guttered — then flared silver.

A scream came from the eastern wing.

They ran.

The Hall of Mirrors, sealed earlier that day, stood open once again — only now, every mirror along its walls had cracked. Some had exploded entirely, shards suspended in the air as if frozen in time.

In the center of the hall stood Professor Corren, her hand raised, her expression strained. "Get back to your dorms," she commanded. But her voice trembled.

Stephen saw it then — the cause. A single mirror at the end of the hall was *bleeding*. Thick, black liquid ran down its surface, pooling at her feet.

Kael whispered, "That's not glass anymore."

Before Corren could react, the mirror *burst*. A shadowed shape erupted outward, like smoke given form. It screamed — not in pain, but in release.

Corren raised her hand to cast, but the shadow struck her full-force, flinging her against the far wall.

Without thinking, Stephen stepped forward. "Kael—"

But Kael was already moving. Together they pulled her out of the way as the mirror light flared.
The shadow's form shifted — human, almost, its face blank and shifting like ripples in water.

"Heir of the First," it whispered.
"The mark calls. The Veil remembers."

Stephen's hand ignited in silver light. The mark — the crescent surrounded by seven runes — burned through his skin. The shadow shrieked and recoiled, dissolving into mist.

The hall fell silent except for the sound of rain hammering the roof.

The Headmaster's Warning

The next morning, the Headmaster called them both to his office.
Headmaster Draven was not a man easily rattled, but today the lines on his face were carved deeper.

He regarded them with eyes like flint. "You two seem to have a habit of being in the wrong place at the right time."

Kael started to speak, but Draven raised a hand. "Save your wit, Thane. The Mirrors were sealed for a reason. That seal was not broken by accident."

He stood, turning toward the massive window that overlooked the Cascades. "Something in this mountain has been waking for years. You've simply made it aware you exist."

Stephen frowned. "Then what are the Mirrors showing us?"

Draven's gaze hardened. "Not what's coming — what's *returning.*"

He moved to the desk, sliding a piece of parchment across it. It was old, ink faded, edges frayed.
Seven symbols encircled a single one — a sigil identical to the mark on Stephen's palm.

"The first Everveil sigil," Draven said quietly. "The one used to bind the Door when it was sealed centuries ago. The one only the House of Shadows was ever meant to guard."

Kael muttered, "So we've been living on top of a lock this whole time."

Draven's reply was low. "And something's trying to open it."

The Raven and the Storm

That evening, thunder rolled again across the mountains. Stephen sat by the window, watching lightning flicker across the valley. In the courtyard below, the silver torches burned brighter, their flames twisting toward the sky.

Kael dropped onto the windowsill beside him. "You ever think about leaving?"
Stephen shook his head. "No. I think about *finishing*."

Kael smirked faintly. "You sound like my father."

"Was he a mage?"

Kael stared out into the storm. "Veilguard. Died before I got to ask him why he joined. Maybe I'll find out one day."

Lightning split the clouds. For a moment, a raven silhouette flashed against the light, wings outstretched. It didn't flap — it *hovered*, suspended in the stormlight before vanishing.

Stephen's mark burned again, stronger than before. "It's happening again," he whispered.

Kael grabbed his shoulder. "Then whatever's waking up — we wake up faster."

Chapter X — The Door Beneath the Veil

The rain had finally stopped, but the quiet it left behind was worse.
Everveil held its breath.

The Hall of Mirrors was sealed once more — this time by the Headmaster himself, with seven sigils burned into the door. Still, whispers spread like wildfire: students claiming to have seen shadows moving under the glass, reflections that didn't match, voices calling their names from the walls.

Stephen tried to ignore it.
But the mark on his hand hadn't stopped burning.

The Warning in the Library

Three days after the incident, Stephen and Kael met again in the lower library, a place few students visited. The lamps here burned blue, their smoke rising in twisting patterns that clung to the vaulted ceiling. The shelves themselves seemed older than the school, carved from the same black stone as the mountain.

Kael was halfway through a forbidden text titled *Echoes of the First Veil* when he looked up.
"Headmaster Draven's been sending Veilguard patrols outside the walls," he whispered. "They're calling it a precaution."

Stephen closed his book. "Precautions don't seal doors with seven sigils."

Kael leaned closer, his tone low. "You think the shadow you saw was… from the other side?"

Before Stephen could answer, the lanterns flickered. One by one, the blue flames went dark — until only the center lamp remained. Its light stretched down the nearest aisle, landing on a section of floor neither of them had ever noticed.

A faint shimmer.

Stephen knelt, brushing dust aside. "There's something carved here."

It was a circle of runes — faded but still pulsing faintly with silver light. Around its edge were seven symbols. One matched the mark on his hand.

Kael crouched beside him. "You've got to be kidding me."

When Stephen placed his palm against the sigil, the runes ignited. The entire library seemed to *breathe.*

Then, the floor split open.

The Descent

A spiral staircase revealed itself, descending deep beneath the mountain. Cold air rushed upward, carrying the scent of stone, water, and old magic.

Kael stared into the darkness. "You know we shouldn't—"

"Yeah," Stephen said. "That's why we have to."

They descended in silence, the only sound their footsteps and the occasional whisper of air through unseen cracks. The deeper they went, the more the walls began to change — carved runes became murals, murals became moving shadows. The stone itself seemed alive, breathing faintly beneath their touch.

At the bottom, the passage opened into a massive circular chamber. In the center stood a black monolith, tall and narrow, inscribed with runes that glowed faint blue.

Kael's voice echoed softly. "Is that… a door?"

Stephen nodded slowly. "The one Draven mentioned."

The Voice Beyond

As they approached, the mark on Stephen's palm began to thrum again — slow, rhythmic, like a second heartbeat. Shadows swirled across the floor, drawn toward the stone.

Kael gripped his shoulder. "Wait. Something's moving inside it."

A faint light pulsed from within the monolith, then a whisper filled the chamber — deep and ancient.

"The blood returns to the gate… The heir awakens the chain…"

The runes flared. The air itself vibrated.

Stephen stumbled back, clutching his hand as the mark bled light. "It's answering me—"

Kael grabbed him. "Then shut it up!"

But before either could react, the monolith cracked.

For a moment, it was only sound — a low hum that rattled their bones. Then came the light: black and silver, twisting into a vortex that clawed at the air.

Something moved inside the crack. Not a figure, but a *presence.*

"The door remembers."

Kael pulled Stephen backward. "We're leaving. Now."

They sprinted up the staircase as the chamber roared behind them. The last thing Stephen saw before the floor sealed shut again was a hand — pale and spectral — pressing against the inside of the door.

The Headmaster's Fury

They were summoned before Draven at dawn. His expression was colder than stone.
"You broke a seal that predates this school by centuries," he said.

Stephen spoke quietly. "The seal found *me.*"

Draven's gaze burned. "Do not mistake fate for invitation. The door beneath the Veil is older than your bloodline, Umbra. Touch it again without my leave and I will seal *you* along with it."

Kael stepped forward. "He didn't mean to—"

"I know what he meant," Draven interrupted. "Now go. And pray the Veil hasn't noticed what you've done."

The Sky Over Everveil

That night, Stephen lay awake, staring at the ceiling. The mountain groaned faintly beneath him — alive, breathing, restless.

Kael's words from earlier echoed in his head.

"You ever think the Veil's not keeping something out… but keeping us in?"

Outside, lightning flickered silently through the clouds.
And deep beneath the school, the door pulsed once more.

A heartbeat.
Waiting.

Chapter XI — The Whispers in the Walls

The days after the library incident passed in uneasy quiet. Classes resumed. Lanterns burned again in the corridors. The students whispered, but none dared to speak Stephen's name too loudly — not after the Headmaster's decree.

Everveil had returned to its rhythm.
But something beneath that rhythm was wrong.

The First Whispers

Stephen first heard it during Spellcraft Theory.

Professor Veyra was lecturing about the alignment of runic frequencies when the world tilted slightly — not in the physical sense, but *inward.* The sound of her voice seemed to stretch thin, replaced by something faint and cold that pressed against the edge of his hearing.

"You opened the door…"

He froze.

Across the classroom, Kael shot him a look — the same frozen awareness mirrored in his eyes. The same whisper, the same intrusion.

When class ended, they lingered behind, pretending to check their notes until the last student left.

"You heard it too," Kael muttered.

Stephen nodded. "It wasn't a person."

"No," Kael said. "It was *Everveil.*"

Echoes of the Veil

That night, they met again in the North Courtyard. Rain misted softly, the torches burning low. The mountains loomed like giants in the dark, their peaks hidden behind cloud.

Kael had brought a small mirror — an old artifact from the Hall incident, half-cracked but still humming with residual energy.

He set it down on the wet stone. "If the door's calling, it'll use reflections again."

Stephen knelt opposite him. "You really think it's… conscious?"

Kael hesitated. "I think Everveil's built on top of something that is."

The mirror's surface rippled. For a moment, Stephen saw only his reflection. Then, a shadow *moved* behind him in the glass — not his, but something taller, broader, its eyes two silver points of light.

"Blood calls to blood…" the voice murmured.

The glass spidered with cracks. Kael snatched it up, hurling it against the wall. It shattered, the pieces scattering across the courtyard like shards of ice.

"Next time," he breathed, "we tell someone."

Stephen looked toward the mountains. "And say what? That the school's talking to us?"

The Headmaster's Visit

The next morning, they were summoned again.

Headmaster Draven waited for them in his office — a chamber lined with relics and tomes that pulsed faintly with stored magic. Behind him, a massive window overlooked the valley, sunlight cutting through the fog like a blade.

"I warned you not to touch the seals," he said evenly.

Stephen straightened. "We didn't. But something's happening."

Draven's eyes flicked toward Kael. "You've both been hearing things?"

"Yes, sir," Kael said. "Voices — same tone as the one from the chamber."

Draven leaned back in his chair, the leather creaking softly. "Then you should know this: once the Veil speaks to you, it doesn't stop. It remembers its heirs."

"Heirs?" Stephen asked.

Draven's gaze lingered on him. "Your bloodline carries something the rest of us were never meant to wield. If the Veil has begun to stir, then your time here will not be peaceful."

He rose, crossing to the window. "Stay out of the lower wings. And if you hear the whispers again — do not answer."

The Cracks in the Stone

That night, the whisper returned.
This time, it came from the walls themselves.

Stephen sat up in bed, breath shallow. Across the dorm, Kael stirred, half-asleep. The sound was soft — like wind through stone, layered with fragments of words.

He slipped out of bed and crossed to the window.

Outside, Everveil's courtyard was empty, the torches guttering low. But on the far wall, beneath the carved sigil of the Institute, the stone itself was *cracking*. Faint blue light seeped through the fissures.

Kael joined him, eyes wide. "That's under the North Hall."

The crack pulsed — once, twice. Then, a small shard of stone fell away, revealing the faint outline of a rune beneath the surface.

It was the same mark burned into Stephen's hand.

The whisper returned, louder now, shaping itself into something like speech:

"The door remembers its blood."

Kael took a step back. "We need to tell Draven."

Stephen didn't move. He reached out, fingers brushing the glowing rune.
The mark on his hand flared in answer.

The light from the wall surged outward, racing across the courtyard — branching, splitting, connecting.

The Veil was waking.

Chapter XII — Embers Beneath Stone

Morning came pale and heavy, like a sky that hadn't slept. Everveil's bells tolled thrice, each note echoing down the misted courtyards. The mountain wind bit sharper than usual, carrying the scent of damp stone and faint ozone.

Stephen walked beside Kael toward the central quad, every step crunching over frost. The other students moved in clusters, murmuring about the same thing — the light, the tremor, the sound that had woken half the dorms.

The Veilguard had sealed off the northern wall before sunrise.

The Summoning

They were summoned by midday.

Professor Valeith awaited them in the observatory — a room of glass and iron high above the towers, where the stars were etched into the dome like constellations of silver flame. She stood beside the Headmaster, her crimson robes whispering as she moved. Her eyes glimmered like embers.

"You touched the mark again," Valeith said. It wasn't a question.

Stephen hesitated. "I didn't mean to. It—"

"—responded," she finished, folding her arms. "It's what the Veil does when it recognizes its own."

Headmaster Draven stepped closer, his expression unreadable. "Professor Valeith specializes in the sealing orders that first bound the Veil. She's here because you've stirred one."

Kael frowned. "The mark's been there for centuries. Why react now?"

Valeith's lips curved faintly, not in amusement but in grim knowledge. "Because something has weakened the bindings. Whatever your ancestors sealed beneath Everveil is no longer dormant."

The Shattered Sigil

They descended into the courtyard together under escort. The Veilguard had cordoned the area with barriers of faint blue light, the sigil still pulsing weakly beneath the cracked wall.

Valeith approached it with cautious reverence. Her gloved hand hovered just above the surface. "This isn't just a wall," she murmured. "It's a vessel. A convergence point for the Veil's energy. And now it's bleeding."

Stephen's mark flared faintly again — a soft silver glow pulsing with the same rhythm as the wall.

Valeith turned to him sharply. "You're bound to it. The wall recognizes your line."

Draven's gaze darkened. "The Umbra line hasn't been touched by the Veil since Erebus himself. Are you suggesting—"

"I'm suggesting it never truly broke the bond," Valeith interrupted. "It's merely been waiting for the right blood to answer."

Kael stepped between them. "So what happens now?"

Valeith exhaled slowly. "Now, we prepare. If the Veil's responding to him, others will feel it soon — and not all will see it as a warning."

The Gathering Shadows

That night, Stephen couldn't sleep. He lay awake listening to the hum beneath the floorboards — the faint, rhythmic pulse that now seemed to echo his heartbeat.

In the darkness, Kael's voice broke the silence. "You ever think about leaving? Just… walking away from all this?"

Stephen turned his head. "And go where? The Veil doesn't stop calling just because I stop listening."

Kael nodded, staring at the ceiling. "Yeah. Guess that's what scares me."

A long silence followed.

Then, somewhere deep beneath the school, the sound of grinding stone echoed through the night.

The hum stopped.

And for a heartbeat — everything was still.

Then the floor trembled again, subtly this time, like something shifting its weight in sleep.

The Veil was stirring beneath Everveil.

Chapter XIII — Whispers Beneath the Veil

The morning after the awakening carried an unease that words couldn't touch.
Even the air felt wrong — as though the mountain itself had been holding its breath since the night before.

Classes resumed, but the rhythm of Everveil had changed. Students whispered in corners. Professors spoke in tones too careful to be casual. Veilguard patrols doubled in the halls, their armor faintly gleaming with sigil-light.

Stephen sat through his morning lectures distracted, watching the sunlight ripple across the rune-etched windows. It had begun to react differently now — light bending faintly toward shadow, colors dulling around him. When his eyes drifted to Kael's, he knew the other boy noticed too.

The Interrogation

By midday, the Headmaster called for him.

The Headmaster's chamber was dim, its only light coming from the crystal orbs that floated above the desk. Draven stood behind it, arms crossed. Beside him, Valeith waited, silent as carved flame.

"Do you understand what you've done?" Draven asked, voice measured.

Stephen hesitated. "I didn't mean to—"

"No one ever does," Draven interrupted. His gaze softened slightly. "The Veil reacts to blood, not intention. You've awakened something dormant, Umbra — and the school is feeling it."

Valeith stepped forward. "There are records," she said quietly. "Writings about the First Veilwalker. About how his descendants could resonate with the sealed places of power. If that's true, then this is only the beginning."

Draven's expression darkened. "Which means we must be ready. I'm reinstating the Night Wards. Valeith, you'll oversee containment. And you"—his eyes turned to Stephen—"will report directly to me from now on. No exceptions."

Stephen nodded. "Yes, Headmaster."

"Good," Draven said. "Because whatever lies beneath this school has just remembered your name."

Echoes of Blood

Later, in the House of Shadows common hall, Kael found him sitting near the fire, silent.

"So," Kael said, dropping into the chair beside him, "did they threaten to expel you, or just haunt you for life?"

Stephen gave a faint smirk. "Neither. They just made it official — I'm apparently related to a cosmic prison."

Kael grinned. "That explains your whole 'brooding over nothing' look."

The humor didn't last long. The firelight dimmed slightly — a ripple in the Veil's energy brushing the edge of perception. Both boys felt it.

Stephen turned toward the wall. "It's growing stronger."

Kael leaned forward, whispering, "Then maybe it's trying to tell us something."

The Mirror Room

That night, the call came again — faint and pulsing beneath the floorboards.
Stephen rose quietly from bed, the glow under his skin tracing faint silver lines along his wrist.

Kael followed without a word.

They moved through the sleeping halls, shadows bending unnaturally as if watching. The sound guided them toward the old section of the school — the abandoned lower halls beneath the observatory, sealed since the Fire Collapse decades ago.

There, behind a cracked mirror framed in black iron, Stephen felt it: the pulse.
The same rhythm as the Veil's hum.

Kael pressed his hand to the mirror's surface. "You feel that?"

Stephen nodded. "It's not a wall… it's a door."

The reflection flickered — for a moment showing not them, but something else.
A staircase spiraling down into darkness.

And then, just as quickly, it was gone.

They exchanged a look.

Kael smirked faintly. "Well, I guess we found what we weren't supposed to find."

Stephen exhaled. "Tomorrow night. We come back prepared."

And beneath the mirror, the sigil of the House of Shadows pulsed once — as if it had been listening all along.

Chapter XIV — The Mirror's Descent

The next day passed in uneasy silence.

Classes continued, but Stephen barely heard a word. Every flicker of shadow along the walls felt like a whisper, every reflection a watchful eye. Even the air seemed charged with anticipation — as if the Institute itself was waiting for him to move.

Kael caught up to him after dinner.
"Still thinking about it, aren't you?"

Stephen looked up from his untouched meal. "You saw it too. That wasn't a reflection. That was a passage."

Kael leaned close, lowering his voice. "Then we go tonight. Before anyone else does."

Stephen hesitated only a moment. "Meet me at the Hall of Echoes. Midnight."

The Descent

The Hall of Echoes was silent when they arrived, moonlight slanting through the arched windows and pooling across the floor like liquid silver. Dust drifted in the air, catching faint glimmers of light from the sigils carved into the columns.

They made their way to the lower corridors. Each step downward felt heavier, the warmth of the school fading into something colder — ancient air that hadn't been disturbed in decades.

At the end of the corridor stood the mirror, waiting.

The crack that had once been faint now glowed with soft white light. Shadows rippled behind the glass, swirling like smoke caught in windless air.

Kael drew a breath. "You ready?"

"No," Stephen said, "but I think that's the point."

He pressed his hand to the mirror.
The surface rippled — liquid and cool — then swallowed them whole.

The Chamber Beneath

They fell through light and darkness both, until the sensation of falling stopped.
When Stephen opened his eyes, they stood in a vast circular chamber.

The floor was carved with seven sigils — one for each House — their lines glowing faintly beneath a web of runes. At the center rose a stone dais shaped like an open eye. On its surface sat a single black book, bound in shadow-thread and sealed with wax.

Kael whispered, "This… this can't be part of the school."

Stephen stepped forward. The closer he got, the stronger the pull became — the same rhythm as the mirror, as his blood. The book responded to him, faint light tracing the Umbra sigil across its cover.

He reached out, and the seal broke with a sound like shattering glass.

The room trembled.
The sigils flared.
And the shadows whispered — not in words, but in thoughts:

The heirs awaken. The blood remembers.

Kael stumbled back. "Stephen, what did you do?"

Before Stephen could answer, the entire floor shifted.
Shadows surged upward like a tide, forming pillars, faces,
hands — reaching toward them. The light from the sigils
began to dim.

Stephen shouted, "Run!"

They barely made it back to the mirror before the chamber
imploded, collapsing inward like a dying star. When they burst
through the other side, they hit the stone corridor gasping for
air.

Behind them, the mirror cracked once more — this time from
within.
A faint pulse echoed through the floor.
And deep beneath the school, something stirred.

Aftermath

They said nothing on the way back to the dorms. Kael's face
was pale, his usual humor stripped away.

Finally, as they reached the staircase to the House of Shadows,
he spoke.
"You're not telling Draven about this, are you?"

Stephen shook his head. "Not yet. Not until we understand what it is."

Kael nodded slowly. "Then whatever happens next… we face it together."

Stephen glanced toward the distant sound of the Veil's hum. "Yeah. Together."

House of
Shadows

Phoenix
rising

Radiant
sun—

House
of tides

House of
Storms

House of
Light

Chapter XV — Whispers in the Halls

The next morning, Everveil woke uneasy.

The sky above the Cascades hung unnaturally still — clouds unmoving, light dimmer than dawn should allow. Students whispered of flickering lamps, of reflections that didn't match their movements, of the sudden drop in temperature that crept through every corridor.

Stephen said nothing. Neither did Kael.
They had sworn the night before that no one could know.

Yet the school already seemed to know.

The Tremor

In *Shadework Theory*, Master Velin's chalk broke mid-stroke. The room trembled — not violently, but with a deep, resonant hum that set the floorboards quivering. Every lamp flickered, throwing shadows against the walls like living things.

Stephen's pulse matched the rhythm. *The blood remembers.*

He caught Kael's glance across the room. The same thought passed silently between them.

Velin frowned, trying to regain order. "Remain seated! It's merely… structural fatigue. The mountains shift often."

But Stephen knew better. The mountain hadn't moved.
The *Veil* had.

The Warning

That evening, the headmaster called a gathering. Students filled the Grand Hall — the high arches of blackened stone echoing with murmurs and nervous laughter. Headmaster Draven stood at the dais, his robes trimmed with silver runes that glowed faintly under the torchlight.

"There has been… a disturbance," he began. "The Veil has rippled — faintly, but unmistakably. It may be a fluctuation caused by the coming solstice, or…"

He hesitated. That pause told the truth before his words did.

"…or it may be that something old has begun to stir beneath us."

The torches dimmed slightly, as if to punctuate his words.

Kael muttered under his breath, "You think he knows?"

Stephen whispered back, "If he did, he'd have shut the lower halls by now."

Draven continued, "Until we are certain, all lower corridors are off limits. Any breach of this order will result in immediate suspension of study — or worse."

The students murmured.
Stephen and Kael exchanged a look that said the same thing: *too late.*

The Shadows Shift

That night, as the two returned to their dormitory, Stephen noticed something strange. His own shadow lagged behind his steps. When he paused, it took a moment to catch up. When he turned, it seemed to stare back at him — just slightly off, just *wrong*.

Kael stopped as well. "Tell me I'm not seeing that."

"You're seeing it," Stephen said quietly.

The shadows along the walls began to thicken — not moving closer, but *watching*. The flicker of lamplight warped them into silent observers, the unseen heartbeat of the school echoing beneath their feet.

Then, from the darkness of the corridor, came a whisper neither could place:

You broke the seal.

Both froze.

Kael's hand went to the dagger at his belt, though steel would mean little here. "Stephen," he whispered, "please tell me that was the wind."

But Stephen didn't answer.
Because he knew the voice.

It was the same that had spoken beneath the earth — the same that had whispered from the book when it opened.

The heirs awaken.

The Choice

Kael grabbed his arm. "We have to tell someone. Draven, Velin — anyone."

Stephen shook his head. "No. Not until we understand it."

"What if it understands us first?"

Stephen glanced toward the window, where the moon hung fractured in the mist. "Then we find out what it wants."

They didn't speak again that night.
But when Stephen slept, he dreamed of the chamber — not ruined as before, but whole again, the sigils burning like suns. And in the center stood a figure cloaked in shadow, holding the black book.

When it turned, he saw his own eyes staring back.

Chapter XVI — The Chamber Beneath the Veil

For three days, the whispers persisted.

They came in fragments — carried on windless air, seeping through cracks in the walls. Sometimes they echoed through mirrors. Sometimes they spoke from the corners of the room when no one was there. Always the same phrase, repeated in a dozen tongues.

The seal is broken. The heir has stirred.

Stephen tried to bury himself in study, but the words followed him. His books turned brittle under his fingers, the ink smearing into unfamiliar sigils when the light dimmed.

Kael, sharper in his instincts, noticed something else — the school was *watching them back.*

The Shift in the Veil

On the fourth night, Master Velin canceled all evening lectures. A faint tremor rippled through the mountain that housed Everveil, strong enough to rattle chandeliers and wake the echoing bells in the northern tower.

The next morning, Headmaster Draven doubled the number of sentinels patrolling the halls — silent figures in shadow-black armor. The Veilguard.

They passed Stephen and Kael in the corridor, faceless behind their masks. Yet as they moved by, the torches dimmed again.

Kael muttered, "That's the third patrol in an hour. Either someone's lost control of a summoning, or—"

"—or they think someone's found something they shouldn't have," Stephen finished.

Their eyes met. They didn't need to say what both were thinking.

The book.

The Descent

By nightfall, the whispers grew stronger.

They led them again to the forbidden lower corridors. The marble floors there were colder than the air itself, every breath misting like frost. Stephen's candle flame flickered blue as they descended.

Kael's hand brushed the wall, tracing ancient grooves beneath the stone. "These aren't cracks. They're wards — old ones. Veilbinding sigils."

Stephen stopped. The markings pulsed faintly under their light. "They're *alive.*"

"Or waking up," Kael murmured.

At the corridor's end, the stone split open — a fissure that hadn't been there before. From within came a faint, rhythmic sound: *thump, thump, thump* — like a heartbeat.

Stephen's pulse synced to it. His candle went out.

The Heart of the Shadow

They entered a cavern vast enough to swallow the entire upper courtyard. The air shimmered with threads of silver mist, coiling like veins through the rock.

And there, suspended above a dais of obsidian, was the *Heart of the Shadow* — a sphere of light and darkness twisting together like storm and flame. Runes spiraled around it, forming a circle of seven sigils — the symbols of the Houses.

Kael took a step forward. "It's beautiful…"

Stephen whispered, "It's alive."

The shadows along the walls stirred, rippling outward like black silk. A voice — deep, resonant, impossibly ancient — filled the chamber.

The heirs awaken. The pact begins anew.

Both froze.

Stephen felt something burn against his chest — the small silver pendant his mother had given him on his fifteenth birthday. It blazed with light, reflecting the sigils on the dais.

Kael shielded his eyes. "Stephen, it's reacting to you!"

The sigils flared, one after another. The chamber quaked. The Heart pulsed brighter — until all went dark.

The Vision

Stephen stood in silence.

No chamber. No torchlight. Only void.

From the darkness emerged seven figures — cloaked in shadow, their faces hidden, their eyes glowing faint silver.

The foremost spoke.

Umbra of the First Shadow, child of the broken line... You have reawakened the Oath.

Stephen tried to speak, but no sound came.

The figure raised a hand. *Seven shall rise when the Veil trembles — heirs of light and dark, bound by vow and blood. The world has forgotten what you are. You must remind it.*

Then the world shattered into light.

The Awakening

Stephen gasped awake on the cavern floor. Kael knelt beside him, shaking his shoulder.

"You stopped breathing," Kael said. His voice trembled — and not from fear alone. "What did you see?"

Stephen stared up at the sigils still faintly glowing above. "The beginning," he whispered.

The shadows along the walls began to twist again — not hostile, not alive, but *listening*.

Kael stood slowly. "I think we just changed everything."

Stephen looked toward the Heart of the Shadow, which now pulsed faintly — a heartbeat once more. "No," he said softly. "*It* changed us."

Chapter XVII — The Echo in the Veil

The mountain did not sleep that night.

By dawn, the air above Everveil shimmered faintly, rippling like heat over glass. Students whispered of strange lights seen from their dormitory windows — silver streaks weaving through the mist that veiled the northern cliffs.

The headmasters called it "residual ward interference."
But those who walked the lower halls felt something deeper: the walls themselves *breathing*.

The Morning After

Stephen woke to a sound like rain — but when he opened his eyes, the ceiling of his dormitory was dry. The sound came from beneath his skin.

When he sat up, faint shadows crawled along his arms like living ink, reacting to his breath. They vanished when Kael entered the room.

"You didn't sleep either," Kael said, closing the door behind him. His own eyes looked darker — not tired, but *different,* the faintest silver hue reflecting light.

Stephen tried to steady his heartbeat. "Whatever we saw down there… it's still here."

Kael tossed him a small stone. "You're telling me. This was in my pocket when I woke up."

The stone pulsed faintly — the same rhythm as the Heart's pulse in the cavern. Stephen's own pendant responded with a subtle glow.

Unrest in the Halls

By midday, the entire Institute seemed restless. Runes flickered along corridor walls. The bell tower's chimes rang hours apart, each echo slightly delayed — as though the sound itself passed through two worlds before reaching them.

Classes were canceled.

Master Velin, head of the House of Shadows, stood before the gathered students in the Hall of Sigils. His voice was calm, but his eyes betrayed unease.

"Something ancient has stirred beneath us," he said. "The wards are holding, but we must remain disciplined. The Veil bends to emotion — and chaos feeds it faster than power."

Kael leaned toward Stephen and muttered, "He's talking about *us.*"

Stephen didn't answer. He could feel the shadows near the hall's pillars reacting to him — tilting, leaning, *listening.*

The Forbidden Library

That night, unable to rest, the two slipped away again — this time to the upper wings of the library. It was older than the main hall, built when Everveil was first founded. Few entered it now; its books were sealed with runic locks and shadow wards.

Kael traced a sigil on one of the heavy iron doors. "This one's marked *Veil Theory: Pre-Division Era.* That's before the clans split."

Stephen's pendant glimmered again. The seal broke with a faint whisper.

Inside, the library was silent — unnaturally so. The air shimmered faintly, and between the shelves, shadows swayed like curtains in a nonexistent breeze.

Books lay open on the tables — though no one had been here in years. One of them, bound in pale leather, bore the mark of the Umbra Clan: a black crescent crossed by a single silver line.

Stephen froze.

Kael stepped beside him. "That's your family's crest."

The book's title glowed faintly: *"Of the First Walker — and the Birth of the Veil."*

The Truth Buried Beneath

They turned the pages carefully.

The text was fragmented, written partly in Old Umbrian — the language of the clans before the schism. But enough could be understood. It spoke of a man who walked between worlds — the First Umbra — whose shadow split from his body and became the Veil itself. A living barrier to hold back what should never be seen.

Kael's voice lowered. "It says the Veil isn't a wall. It's a wound."

Stephen's eyes flicked to a passage inked in red. *When the wound reopens, the bloodline shall call it home.*

Before either could speak, a deep hum rolled through the air. The candles dimmed. From between the shelves, shadows rose again — not mist, but figures.

Tall, hooded, silent. Watching.

Kael reached for the small stone, which began to burn in his palm. "Stephen…"

The air twisted.

The largest of the figures spoke, voice hollow as wind through a crypt:
You have read the forbidden name. The Oath has begun its return.

Stephen's pendant flared once more — white light cutting through the dark. The figures recoiled, fading back into the shelves.

When silence fell, only the echo of their words remained.

Kael whispered, "We're in this now, aren't we?"

Stephen closed the book, the mark of the Umbra crest still glowing faintly on its cover. "We always were."

Chapter XVIII — The Shadow That Answers

The night after their discovery, the rain would not stop.
It fell not from the clouds, but from the Veil itself — a slow,
steady descent of black mist that drifted through Everveil's
courtyards and bled into the cracks between stones.

Students awoke to find words scrawled across their mirrors
and windows — words that vanished when read aloud. The
Headmasters locked the upper floors, sealed the lower vaults,
and declared an immediate curfew.

Only those of the House of Shadows were still permitted to
move freely.

Stephen and Kael, though barely students, found themselves
summoned to the Hall of Echoes.

The Hall of Echoes

The hall was vast and circular, its walls lined with iron mirrors
that reflected nothing. The Head of House, Master Velin,
stood before the great sigil carved into the floor — the
crescent entwined with the wolf's head of Umbra.

"Something ancient has awakened below," he said. His voice
was even, but the air trembled. "Our wards are trembling. You
were seen in the Forbidden Library last night."

Stephen swallowed. "We found a book — about the First
Umbra. About the Veil being—"

"A wound." Velin finished for him. "Yes. That text was not meant for your eyes."

Kael shifted uneasily. "Then why was it open? Why did it react to him?"

Velin's gaze flicked to Stephen. "Because his blood remembers."

Before Stephen could answer, the sigil in the floor began to glow — first faintly, then fiercely, threads of silver fire crawling up from the cracks. The mirrors vibrated. Shadows peeled from their surfaces like smoke given form.

Velin turned sharply. "The Veil is thinning *now!* Everyone out!"

But Stephen couldn't move. The pendant at his neck pulsed in rhythm with the floor's light, anchoring him. He felt the world split around him — one half here, one half somewhere beyond.

The Rift Opens

The light tore itself open.
A black wind howled through the chamber, and from its center, a shape began to emerge — a silhouette first, then form: a wolf, vast and silver-eyed, half mist and half flesh.

Its voice was not heard but *felt.*
Umbra blood... born again.

Velin drew his blade of silver flame. "It's a specter! Contain it!"

But the wolf's gaze fell on Stephen — and every other light in
the room died.

The next moment, Stephen stood alone in darkness.

The creature towered before him, its fur rippling with starlight.
"You are not ready," it said.
"I didn't call you."
"You didn't have to."

The wolf stepped closer, the ground beneath its paws melting
into liquid shadow.
"The First Walker bound me to your line. I am the shape of
what walks between. The day you accept the Veil, you accept
me."

Stephen's voice trembled. "And if I don't?"

Its eyes flared white.
"Then it will accept you — and you will no longer be human."

The vision shattered.

Aftermath

Stephen gasped, collapsing onto the cold stone. The hall was
in ruins — mirrors shattered, runes burned into the walls. Kael
knelt beside him, blood on his forehead. "You stopped
breathing. What the hell was that?"

Stephen's hand shook. "It was… a wolf. Not just a vision — it
knew me."

Velin approached, leaning heavily on his staff. "Then the old stories were true. The Familiar of the First Bloodline… the one who survived the Sundering."

He looked at Stephen gravely. "It seems your bond has already begun."

Kael stared between them. "Bond? What bond?"

Velin sighed. "Every true-born of the Shadow Line finds their reflection — their living echo — a creature born of their soul. Yours has chosen early."

Stephen met Kael's gaze, the memory of silver eyes still burning in his mind.
"I didn't choose it," he said quietly.
Kael grinned faintly despite the tension. "Maybe it chose right."

Chapter XIX — The Bond of Shadow and Silver

The rain had ceased, but the mist refused to leave.
It clung to Everveil like a memory — a quiet, persistent breath that wound through its arches and towers, curling around every lantern and broken shard of last night's storm.

Stephen sat upon the edge of his narrow bed, the world still trembling around him. His shadow burned faintly on the wall, stretched too far — alive, though he wished it weren't.

In the corner, half-substantial and yet impossibly real, the **wolf** slept.
Ashael.

It was not merely an animal. Its form flickered between flesh and vapor, every breath a shimmer of silver light swallowed by shadow. Its ribs rose and fell slowly, like waves on a black sea. Occasionally, its eyes opened — twin moons caught in smoke — and Stephen felt his pulse match the creature's.

He hadn't slept since the summoning. Every time his eyes closed, he saw through Ashael's.
Every time he breathed, he felt something ancient move beneath his skin.

The Summons

A knock at the door shattered the silence.
Kael stood there — disheveled, his hair still damp from the morning fog, his expression caught somewhere between worry and awe.

"They're calling you to the upper council," he said, voice hushed but heavy. "The entire school's talking about it. Half of them think you opened the Veil yourself."

Stephen managed a weak smile. "I didn't open it. It opened for me."

Kael snorted softly. "Doesn't make it better."

They crossed the courtyard in silence. The mist hung low, wrapping the cobblestones and the gothic bridges between the towers. Everveil's spires groaned faintly in the wind, the sound of an ancient beast stirring in its sleep.

By the time they reached the **Hall of Seven**, two Veilguard soldiers waited — cloaked in black and silver armor, faces expressionless.

"Stephen Umbra," one of them said. "You are summoned before the Council of Masters."

Kael stepped forward. "Then I'm coming too."

The guards exchanged glances but said nothing.

The Hall of Seven

The chamber of the Seven was vast, its ceiling a mirror of obsidian etched with sigils that pulsed faintly in rhythm with the mountain's heart. Seven banners hung in a perfect circle, each bearing the crest of a House — Flame, Stone, Storms, Tides, Light, Mind, and Shadows.

At the center stood a raised dais of black marble veined with silver. Upon it, the **Archmaster, Seraith Vale**, waited — tall, robed in gray and silver. Her eyes were pale as frost, her hands clasped behind her back.

Around her stood the other six Heads, each one a pillar of mastery, their faces lined with years and burden. But none bore the mark of a Familiar. They were scholars, wardens, and wielders of ancient rites — the guardians of Everveil's law, not its living power.

When Stephen entered, the temperature seemed to shift. The torches dimmed.
Ashael followed in silence, silver eyes gleaming from the mist behind him.

The Heads collectively recoiled — not out of disgust, but recognition.

Archmaster Seraith's voice cut through the hall.
"Name it."

Stephen swallowed. "Ashael. It came through the rift. It knew my name."

A murmur passed through the circle.

The Head of Storms sneered. "A conjured illusion — shadow-born delusion."

The Head of Mind spoke quietly, fingers resting on his temple. "No illusion knows a mortal's name. It is bound to his soul."

Seraith's gaze was sharp as glass. "A Familiar of the First Bloodline… The Wolf of the Veil."

Kael shifted uneasily beside Stephen. "What does that mean?"

Velin, the dark-eyed Head of Shadows, answered. "It means the Umbra line has awakened again — the first in generations. Such bonds don't form unless the Veil itself is thinning."

Seraith stepped forward. "The creature is not to be destroyed, nor dismissed. It is to be studied — understood — contained if necessary."

Her gaze lingered on Stephen. "You will remain under the supervision of the House of Shadows. Every moment you breathe with it, the Veil watches. Do not give it reason to whisper your name again."

Ashael's ears twitched. Its eyes glowed faintly brighter. The banners above fluttered though there was no wind.

The Heads instinctively stepped back.

Seraith whispered, "So it begins again."

The Bond

That night, Stephen sat by the open window of his dormitory. The moon hung fractured above the mist, painting the valley in liquid silver. Kael leaned against the wall beside him, arms crossed.

"You're not sleeping, are you?"

Stephen shook his head. "Every time I close my eyes, I see through his."

Kael gave a dry laugh. "Lucky you. I only see through my homework."

Ashael stirred from the shadows, padding closer, its paws silent. When it looked at Stephen, he heard a whisper that wasn't sound.

You are not alone.

He flinched slightly.

Kael glanced over. "You all right?"

Stephen nodded slowly. "Yeah… it's just—"
He hesitated. "It spoke."

Kael blinked. "In your head?"

"More like… *through* it."

He looked out at the mountains, where the mist moved like breathing flesh.
"What did it say?" Kael asked.

Stephen smiled faintly, the ghost of awe still caught in his throat.
"That I'm not alone."

Ashael's eyes glimmered once more — and in that moment, far beneath the school, the old seals carved into Everveil's foundations pulsed faintly in response.

The world had noticed.

Chapter XX — Lessons of Containment

The morning fog clung to the valley like breath.
Everveil's towers rose through it, their peaks glimmering faintly in the pale light.
The House of Shadows had fallen into rhythm—lectures by day, duels and meditation by night—but beneath it all, something unspoken moved.

It began with the shadows. They had started to react.

When Stephen walked the marble halls, the torches dimmed slightly, and the air grew cooler. The instructors said it was *attunement*, the result of his blood adjusting to the school's ancient wards.
But Headmaster Velin had called it something else.

"Containment," he'd said. "The shadow inside you listens now. Your task is to make sure it obeys."

The Practice Field

That evening, Stephen stood in the lower courtyard with the other first-years, their black training robes shimmering faintly under the Veillight orbs. Professor Ilyra paced before them, her staff tapping the flagstones in rhythm with her words.

"Focus not on control," she said, "but conversation. Shadow is alive, and it resents a leash. You must make it believe it *wants* to serve you."

A student to Stephen's left failed his attempt; his summoned shadow lashed backward, scattering into smoke. Ilyra didn't even glance his way. She looked at Stephen instead.

"Mr. Umbra. You first."

Stephen stepped forward. He exhaled slowly and extended a hand. The air wavered. The torches dimmed further. From beneath his feet, a ripple of shadow began to form—a trembling pool of liquid black.

He focused his mind on the memory of home: moonlight over Duskford's fields, his father's voice telling him the darkness was not an enemy but an inheritance.

The pool solidified.

For a moment, it took shape—a vague outline of something wolfish, its silver eyes flickering before it dissolved again into mist.

Ilyra tilted her head, her tone almost approving. "Not bad. But you lack containment. You *invited* it; you didn't *anchor* it."

Stephen wiped sweat from his brow. "It's… stronger than I thought."

"It always is," Ilyra said softly. "Shadow rarely serves those who fear their own reflection."

The Lesson Beneath the Lesson

After practice, Kael Thane fell into step beside him. The older boy carried himself with easy confidence, his cloak trailing faint smoke at the edges—a side effect of his own shadowcraft.

"Not bad, Umbra," Kael said with a grin. "You almost made it purr."

Stephen smirked, exhausted. "Is that supposed to be a compliment?"

Kael shrugged. "For the House of Shadows? It's practically a medal."

They reached the edge of the courtyard, where moonlight spilled through a fractured window, casting broken light over the floor.

Kael leaned on the sill. "Just a few days till my birthday," he said, half to himself. "The Veil always feels thinner this time of year."

Stephen glanced over. "You were born near Samhain?"

Kael nodded. "October thirty-first. Guess that explains a lot."

Stephen chuckled. "That it does."

Kael's grin was faint, but it lingered. "Maybe the Veil'll give me something new this year. A sign. A spark. Something that actually makes sense."

"You'd probably just complain about the paperwork," Stephen said.

Kael laughed, the sound echoing softly through the corridor. "Fair."

The Wolf's Mark

That night, unable to sleep, Stephen returned to the training field. The moon hung low and swollen, the air alive with the hum of the Veil.

He knelt at the courtyard's center and summoned the shadow again. This time, he didn't fight it. He *listened*.

The darkness rose up, slow and patient. A shape emerged—a wolf formed entirely of smoke and silver light. Its eyes met his, not as a beast, but as something *remembered*.

"You're not afraid," he whispered.

The creature tilted its head, then stepped forward. When its muzzle touched his hand, heat flooded his veins. He gasped, clutching his wrist.

Lines of light began to trace themselves across his skin— silver, sharp, deliberate. The pattern formed a crescent split by a wolf's eye, the mark pulsing once before cooling into ink.

He stared, breathless.

The air rippled—and the wolf dissolved, fading into his shadow like it had been swallowed by his heartbeat.

A whisper echoed faintly in his mind, soft and steady:
Call, and I will come.

Kael's voice startled him. "You're out here too?"

Stephen turned, hiding the mark. "Couldn't sleep."

Kael squinted. "You've got that look. Something happened."

Stephen hesitated, then raised his arm. The tattoo shimmered under the moonlight.

Kael let out a low whistle. "That wasn't there before."

"No," Stephen said quietly. "But it's mine now."

The mark pulsed again, and for a brief second, a shadow moved at Stephen's feet—a wolf's silhouette, silent and watchful.

Kael grinned. "Guess you found your way to make it obey."

Stephen looked down at the faint glow under his skin. "Not obey," he said softly. "Understand."

The Vinculum Sigil

By morning, the mark had faded to ink, but its warmth remained.

It would not be the last of its kind.
In time, when the others of the Vow found their familiars,
each would bear a sigil—an echo of this moment.
A binding between power and purpose.
A mark that whispered not of ownership, but of **shared will.**

And though none of them yet understood it, the first thread of the **Ebon Vow** had been woven.

Chapter XXI — The Veil of Autumn

The air had turned sharp by the end of October, the mountains cloaked in their first thin layer of frost. Pumpkins carved with faint runes glowed along the lower paths of Everveil, their faces flickering between grins and sigils. The halls smelled faintly of cider and iron—an odd mix of celebration and the quiet reminder that even holidays carried weight in a school built on shadow.

Kael's birthday was in two days, and though he pretended not to care, Stephen could tell otherwise. He'd caught him staring once or twice at the storm-lit horizon beyond the western towers, a faraway look in his eyes.

The Library of Veils

It was raining when they entered the library that evening. Not the soft drizzle of Duskford, but Everveil's cold, silver rain—the kind that shimmered as it fell, like thin strands of liquid light.

Stephen followed Kael through aisles that stretched for what felt like miles. The shelves breathed faintly, wards humming between them like heartbeats.

Kael stopped at a circular table near the back, where a book lay open, its pages rippling in the airless stillness.

"What's that?" Stephen asked.

Kael glanced up. "A registry," he said. "Of every student who's ever stepped through the Veil."

Stephen frowned. "That's not allowed to be read."

Kael smirked. "You're assuming I care."

He turned the page. The parchment was black, the ink silver—names written in looping, ancient script. Each glowed faintly, pulsing with memory.

Stephen leaned in—and the letters moved. His breath caught as one shimmered brighter than the rest.

"Kael Thane," Stephen read aloud.

But below it, a second name flickered—faint, almost erased. "Corvus," he whispered.

Kael froze. "What?"

"It's your name," Stephen said. "Or—what you'll become."

Kael's face paled. "How do you know that?"

"I don't," Stephen said quietly. "The book does."

The candles guttered. A gust of unseen wind swept through the stacks. For a moment, both saw something reflected in the glass of the far window—a bird of smoke, its wings stretched wide before dissolving into mist.

The Eve of Samhain

By the next night, Everveil had transformed.

Lanterns hung from every archway, carved with runes of warding and invitation. Students gathered in the central courtyard for the Samhain Eve festival, where the Headmasters lit the Shadow Pyres—silver flame that burned without smoke.

Stephen stood with Kael near the edge of the crowd, both cloaked in their house colors. The night pulsed with energy—the boundary between the Veil and the world stretched thin.

Kael exhaled. "It's always loud before midnight," he said, staring at the pyres. "But after… the air goes still. Like something's listening."

Stephen nodded. "You think your name in that book means something?"

Kael gave a small laugh. "Everything here means something. We just don't understand it yet."

He reached into his pocket and produced two glass vials of silver liquid. "Found these in the alchemy stores. Shadowglass. They use it for scrying practice. Thought we could try our luck."

"Is this your idea of celebrating?" Stephen asked.

Kael grinned. "We're in the House of Shadows. This *is* celebrating."

They stepped beneath one of the high arches, the roar of the crowd fading behind them. Kael poured the liquid onto the floor between them. It spread like ink, then began to shimmer—mirroring the moon overhead.

The reflection shifted—revealing faint silhouettes of creatures moving on the other side of the veil.

Stephen swallowed hard. "Kael—"

But Kael's expression was calm, almost reverent. "They're watching. They always watch on my birthday."

A gust of wind extinguished the nearby lanterns. The mirror of light and ink quivered—and for an instant, the reflection of the wolf and raven appeared side by side before vanishing into darkness.

The Promise

Later that night, when the courtyard had emptied and the pyres had burned low, Stephen and Kael sat on the stone steps outside the dormitory. Frost had begun to gather on the railing, glowing faintly under the moon.

"You saw it too, didn't you?" Kael asked quietly.

Stephen nodded. "The wolf and the raven."

Kael smiled faintly. "Then I guess we're already linked. Whether we like it or not."

"Seems that way," Stephen said.

Kael leaned back, looking up at the fractured moon. "You ever think maybe the Veil didn't make a mistake with us? That it's just… waiting for us to figure out why we're here?"

Stephen didn't answer. He looked down at the silver lines faintly visible beneath his sleeve—the mark of the wolf pulsing once in the moonlight.

Somewhere beyond the mountain ridge, the midnight bell
tolled twelve times.
Kael's birthday had begun.

And something in the dark stirred to acknowledge it.

Chapter XXII — The Hall of Whispers

The library of Everveil was alive at night.
Not with the noise of students or the creak of old wood, but
with *breathing*—a soft, measured rhythm that pulsed through
the shelves like something asleep beneath the stone.

Stephen had noticed it first.

He and Kael had been finishing a late-night study session—
Kael half-distracted, tossing shadows across the candlelight
with the idle twitch of his fingers, while Stephen tried to focus
on the intricacies of Veil theory. The only sound had been the
scratching of quills, until Stephen's pen had stopped mid-
word.

"Do you hear that?" he whispered.

Kael frowned, lowering his book. "Hear what? The wind?"

Stephen shook his head. "No. It's… under the floor."

Kael smirked. "You mean *ghosts*?"

Stephen didn't answer. He was already on his feet, eyes
tracing the edges of the flagstones. There was something off
about the pattern—one stone darker than the others, the runes
carved faintly but deliberately. It wasn't part of the library's
normal design.

"Help me move this," Stephen said.

Kael sighed, though his grin betrayed curiosity. "If a librarian
catches us, you're explaining."

Together they shifted the heavy wooden table aside. The
candlelight caught on the rune's surface, revealing a faint

shimmer—the outline of a circle carved deep into the floor. Within it, the mark of the seven houses radiated outward, each sigil drawn in fine silver lines. At the center, however, was something different: a crescent of shadow, cut clean through the stone.

Kael's smirk faded. "That's not part of the school's crest."

"No," Stephen murmured. "It's older."

He placed his palm against the crescent. The air grew colder. For a heartbeat, silence overtook the world—and then the rune *breathed*. A pulse of darkness radiated outward, extinguishing every candle in the room.

Kael swore under his breath. "Stephen—what did you—"

The floor opened.

A staircase of pure shadow descended into the earth, vanishing beneath the library. From below came a faint hum—a whispering chorus, distant yet familiar, like voices calling from a dream Stephen had half-forgotten.

Kael hesitated only a moment before grinning again. "Well. After you."

The descent felt endless.

The walls were smooth and seamless, carved from the same black stone as the sigil chamber. Every step echoed faintly, though the air grew thicker the deeper they went, heavy with something that wasn't quite fear—but reverence. A memory of being watched by something ancient.

At the base of the stairway lay a hall—a vast, circular chamber lit by veins of silver that pulsed like veins through living flesh. The symbols of the seven Houses glowed faintly along the outer walls, and between them flowed shadow itself, twisting and reshaping like smoke in a breeze.

And in the center, a ring of obsidian floated an inch above the ground.

Stephen's pulse quickened. "This isn't supposed to exist."

Kael stepped closer, eyes wide. "Then why does it feel like it's been waiting for us?"

The ring began to hum—softly at first, then with growing strength. The sigils along the walls flared, and the shadows rose like living flame, swirling around the two of them. For an instant, Stephen thought he saw shapes within them—wolves, ravens, serpents, and something that resembled the curve of a hand reaching outward.

Then came the *voice*.

"Children of shadow, sons of breath and silence..."
"...the time of the Veil is upon you."

Stephen fell to his knees, clutching his head. The air itself burned against his skin, and a mark seared itself into his right wrist—a spiraling symbol that glowed silver before fading into a faint tattoo, shaped like a wolf's head encircled by crescent light.

Kael stumbled backward, eyes wide. "Stephen—your arm—!"

He barely heard him. The chamber was pulsing now, the shadows retreating, the ring sinking back into the ground as if never there. The air grew still again. Only the faint hum of silence remained.

When Stephen finally looked up, Kael was staring at his own arm. A faint imprint shimmered there, too—not yet formed, but waiting.

"What was that?" Kael whispered.

Stephen's voice was hollow. "A call."

Kael's grin returned, slower this time, edged with awe. "A call to what?"

Stephen met his gaze, eyes reflecting the dying silver light. "To whatever waits beyond the Veil."

The two boys stood in silence as the stairway sealed itself behind them, leaving no trace of the path they had taken. Only the faint scent of burnt silver remained.

Above, the library stood still and quiet once more—yet somewhere in the deep of the school, something ancient had awakened.

Chapter XXIII — The Echo Between Worlds

By morning, neither Stephen nor Kael spoke of what they'd seen.

The library had sealed itself, its floor once again unbroken marble, the sigil erased as though it had never been. And yet, the mark on Stephen's wrist remained — faint, silver in some lights, black in others. Kael's, too, though his seemed dormant, pulsing faintly whenever Stephen drew near.

They'd agreed to tell no one. Not yet.

The days that followed unfolded in eerie calm. Classes resumed — theory of veiling, practical shadowwork, elemental balance — but the air of Everveil had changed. Whispers carried through the halls of the **House of Shadows**, murmurs of strange dreams and flickering candlelight that dimmed when no wind stirred.

Even Headmistress Veyra's tone in assembly had shifted, her eyes lingering longer on the new students as if measuring their weight against some unseen scale.

And though the other Houses carried on as usual, Everveil itself *felt* awake.

Stephen sat in his dorm late one night, moonlight washing over the desk. His notes were open but ignored. He traced the faint lines of his wrist mark with a fingertip. It was cool to the touch, but when he closed his eyes, he could hear a whisper — not a voice exactly, but *memory*, like something old pressing through the edges of thought.

Children of shadow... sons of breath and silence...

He opened his eyes. The candle before him flickered violently. Across the room, Kael stirred in his sleep. The mark on his own wrist shimmered once, then dimmed.

A knock interrupted the silence.

Stephen turned, startled. The hour was too late for visitors. He crossed to the door and cracked it open. A figure stood there in the dim corridor — older, sharp-eyed, and cloaked in the colors of the House of Mind.

"Soren Corren," the boy said, introducing himself before Stephen could speak. "Second year. You're the Umbra boy, aren't you?"

Stephen hesitated, uncertain. "You could just say Stephen."

Soren smirked slightly. "They've been talking about you since the sorting. And about the shadows under the library."

Stephen's blood ran cold. "What did you hear?"

"That they moved," Soren said, lowering his voice. "And that someone—" he glanced down at Stephen's arm, "—woke them."

Before Stephen could reply, another voice came from down the hall.

"Leave him alone, Soren."

Arienna Valeith stepped out from a stairwell, her dark hair tied back, a flicker of candlelight reflected in her eyes. A first-year like Stephen, though her confidence seemed older.

"You're not supposed to be prowling around after curfew," she said, crossing her arms.

Soren gave a mock bow. "Neither are you, flameborn."

"Go haunt someone else," Arienna shot back.

He grinned and retreated, the shadows almost folding behind him as he vanished down the hall.

Stephen blinked. "You know him?"

Arienna sighed. "Everyone knows Soren. He thinks rules are suggestions."

She tilted her head at Stephen. "He's right about one thing, though. You should be careful what you touch here. Everveil's got more doors than anyone knows what to do with."

Stephen tried to answer, but she'd already turned to go, the flicker of her candle trailing like a ribbon of living light behind her.

Later that night, as the silence returned, Stephen lay awake. Kael mumbled in his sleep — words Stephen couldn't quite make out — but the rhythm of his breathing matched the pulse of something deeper.

That whisper again. That same ancient tone.
And this time, Stephen could almost understand it.

"When the shadows breathe, the Veil remembers."

Chapter XXIV — Whispers Beneath the Veil

The next morning, a storm rolled across Lake Crescent.

Rain clung to the glass towers of Everveil, cascading in sheets that blurred the world beyond. The halls were hushed except for the murmurs of students making their way to class, boots wet, cloaks dripping. Thunder echoed across the valley like the sound of drums from a forgotten war.

Stephen sat beside Kael in the lecture hall of the **House of Shadows**, trying to focus on Professor Halwen's voice. The man was ancient, pale-eyed, and spoke as though every word carried centuries of dust.

"Shadow," Halwen said, "is not absence. It is memory. It is what light leaves behind."

He tapped his staff against the slate floor, and a ripple of black mist spiraled upward, forming into a fleeting shape — a wolf's head, fading before it could howl.

"Light reveals," Halwen continued. "But shadow *remembers*. Learn to listen to it, and it will tell you what the world hides."

Stephen's mark burned faintly beneath his sleeve.

At lunch, Kael was quiet — more than usual. He sat across from Stephen in the dining hall, idly stirring a bowl of soup as the wind rattled the stained-glass windows.

"You've been quiet since the library," Kael said finally.

Stephen looked up. "So have you."

"Yeah, but mine's nerves. Yours feels… different. Like it's calling to you."

Stephen opened his mouth to answer but stopped when he felt it — a pulse beneath his skin, subtle but certain. The same hum from that night, like the Veil itself breathing beneath the school.

Kael noticed. "It's happening again, isn't it?"

Stephen nodded slowly.

Across the hall, Arienna entered with a small cluster of first-years from the **House of Flame**. Her gaze flicked to Stephen briefly — and lingered. The flicker of her candlelight had followed her here; it danced around her like a living spark even when no candle was present.

She hesitated, then crossed the hall.

"Stephen," she said quietly, setting her tray beside him. "Professor Valeith wants to see you."

He blinked. "Who?"

"My uncle," she explained. "He's head of the House of Flame — and… he said your name came up in council."

Kael frowned. "Council? Why?"

Arienna lowered her voice. "Because they think you touched something the Veil didn't give permission for."

The room went still around them. For a heartbeat, the sound of the rain filled everything. Then Stephen exhaled.

"Then I should probably find out what they think I did."

The council chamber was deep within the Institute, beneath the oldest tower where the stone walls were etched with shadow-script. Each House sent one head — seven chairs, seven banners, seven old secrets.

Headmistress Veyra sat at the center, her silver hair braided tight like steel wire. Her eyes caught Stephen's as he entered — calm, assessing, and far too knowing.

"Stephen Umbra," she said. "Son of Cael and Elara Umbra. You have come far in a short time."

Stephen inclined his head. "I was told you wanted to see me."

"We did," she said. "Because Everveil does not forget. And last week, in the old library, you awoke something that had not stirred in a century."

One of the other heads — Professor Valeith, tall and fire-eyed — folded his arms. "We have long suspected the lower vaults were sealed by intention, not decay. The Veil moves when its heirs act."

"The mark," Veyra said, glancing at his wrist. "May I?"

Stephen hesitated but extended his hand. The faint sigil shimmered faintly, silver against his skin.

Veyra didn't touch it. She only studied it, her expression unreadable.

"It has chosen you," she murmured. "But choice brings consequence."

He looked up. "What does it mean?"

She leaned back. "It means the Veil remembers your bloodline."

The room dimmed slightly — or maybe it only felt that way.

Valeith spoke again, softer now. "You're not in trouble, boy. But what you've awakened… is older than this school."

Stephen glanced between them. "Then what happens now?"

Veyra's gaze sharpened, her voice cutting through the tension like a blade.
"Now," she said, "you learn *why* it chose you."

That night, Stephen couldn't sleep. The rain had stopped, but the world still whispered. He turned the words of the Headmistress over and over in his head.

When he finally closed his eyes, the dream came.

He stood in a hall of mirrors — each reflection a different version of himself, each carrying a different mark. Shadows moved between them, shifting like living ink.

From the darkness, a voice called — soft, cold, and *familiar*.

"You were born to remember, Stephen Umbra. And soon, the shadows will remember you."

Chapter XXV — Shadows Beneath the Snow

The first snow of winter fell over Everveil like a benediction. The towers were quiet beneath the silver drifts, the forest hushed except for the wind that whispered between the black pines. Classes had ended, and the bells tolled the start of the winter recess — that long-awaited span of days when even the most vigilant professors dared to rest.

Stephen stood beneath the archway of the House of Shadows, his travel cloak dusted with frost. His breath curled in the cold air as he glanced back at the school that had, for the first time in his life, begun to feel like home. Behind him, the banners of the seven Houses swayed in the breeze — faint glimmers of power sleeping beneath the sigils.

Kael trudged up beside him, his own pack slung over his shoulder.
"Hard to believe we survived a whole term," he said with a grin. "Barely."

Stephen smiled faintly. "You mean *you* barely survived."

"I'm telling you, Professor Halwen's practical exams were a setup," Kael muttered. "You can't make us fight our own reflections and call that education."

"That was the point," Stephen replied. "To see what parts of ourselves fight back."

Kael groaned. "And now you sound like Draven. Please stop."

They both laughed — the easy kind that comes when exhaustion and relief blur together. Around them, students hurried to and from the carriages lined along the courtyard, their familiars flitting in the air above the gates. The faint smell of spiced cider and pinewood came from the Great Hall, where the House of Flame had already started their end-of-term feast.

Headmistress Veyra stood near the fountain, her black and silver robes flowing like liquid night. Her eyes followed each departing student with a calm watchfulness that was almost tender — almost.
When Stephen and Kael passed her, she gave a slow nod.

"Homeward, Mr. Umbra?"
"Yes, Headmistress," Stephen replied. "Back to Duskford."

"Good," she said softly. "The Veil stirs strangely this winter. Better to be among your kin while it sleeps."

Her gaze lingered — sharp and thoughtful — before she turned away.

Kael exhaled once they were clear. "Why does she always sound like she's quoting prophecy?"

"Because she probably is," Stephen said, but he was smiling.

The train left just before dusk.

Snow fell thicker as they wound down from the Cascades, cutting through forests that glimmered like frozen glass. The windows of the carriage steamed, and Stephen rested his forehead against the glass, watching the mountains fade into distance. The quiet hum of the rails was almost hypnotic.

Kael dozed off halfway through the journey, a notebook still open on his lap. His writing was full of sketches — the seven

House sigils, the old Veilguard symbol, and half-finished runes that looked like guesses toward something greater. Stephen glanced down at it, wondering how much Kael *really* understood about the power that slept beneath Everveil's halls.

When the train finally pulled into Duskford Station, Stephen stepped out into a swirl of soft white air.
The town hadn't changed.
Lanterns burned in the windows, the cobblestone streets dusted with snow, and smoke curled gently from the chimneys. The world was quieter here — smaller, perhaps — but after the storms of study and shadowcraft, it felt like breathing again.

And standing at the end of the platform, wrapped in heavy coats, were **Cael** and **Elara Umbra**.

His mother's smile was the kind that reached her eyes. His father's was rare and restrained, but no less warm.
"Welcome home, Stephen," Cael said, clasping his shoulder.

Stephen hesitated — then hugged him, the way he had as a child. The scent of soot and pine oil clung to his father's coat, the familiar smell of the forge.

"You've grown," his father murmured.
"You always say that," Stephen replied.
"And every time, it's still true."

Elara's voice came softer, gentler. "You must tell us everything. The Houses, your friends… the shadows."
He smiled. "You'll get tired of hearing about it."

"We'll risk it."

That night, the Umbra house glowed with candlelight and
warmth.
The fire crackled, shadows danced across the walls, and a
familiar comfort settled into Stephen's bones. As his parents
spoke quietly by the hearth, he found himself tracing the faint
pattern of the mark beneath his wrist — the sigil of the Veil
that had appeared when he first stepped into Everveil.

Outside, snow continued to fall.
And somewhere in the dark beyond Duskford, the wind
carried an echo — distant, shifting, almost a whisper.

A reminder that though the world slept, the Veil never truly
did.

Chapter XXVI — Whispers Beneath Winter

The days that followed were steeped in peace.

Snow fell over Duskford like a soft veil, burying the rooftops and muffling the sound of the world. The Umbra home stood at the forest's edge, its windows lit gold against the gray. Inside, the air smelled of pine and old parchment, of his mother's herbal candles and his father's forge still faintly warm from the morning's work.

Stephen sat by the window in his old room — smaller than he remembered — a book open on his lap. It wasn't one from Everveil's library, but rather one his father had written: ***The Nine Veils: A History of Shadowcraft in the Old World.*** He'd read it as a child, back when "shadowcraft" was still a bedtime word — not something that hummed in his veins.

From below, he could hear the familiar rhythm of his parents' voices. Elara was humming softly, and Cael was speaking with the forge-hand, his voice low and steady. The sound of it felt like home — real, grounding.

But something beneath that comfort lingered — a whisper at the edge of hearing.

He glanced at the frost-rimmed window, half expecting to see movement in the treeline. Nothing. Only falling snow.

Then the whisper came again. Not outside — *inside.*
From the mark beneath his wrist. The one that had appeared the day he entered Everveil's gates.

He pressed his fingers to it, feeling the faint pulse of heat under the skin.

"Do you hear it too?"

The voice wasn't his. It wasn't anyone's.
It was a feeling — an echo — like someone speaking from far
away through the cracks between dreams.

He inhaled slowly and whispered back, "Who are you?"

The answer came as a shiver in the spine of the world.

"The bond remembers."

And then — silence.

That evening, as the snow thickened outside, the Umbra
family gathered for dinner. The hearth glowed orange, and
shadows curled along the walls like resting spirits.

Cael poured mulled wine for himself and Elara, while Stephen
nursed a mug of tea that steamed faintly in the firelight. For a
long while, they simply talked — not of power or prophecy,
but of the small things. The forge's new commission. The
market's frost fairs. The fact that the old clock tower finally
froze mid-chime again.

When the conversation shifted, it did so quietly.

"You've changed," Elara said softly.

Stephen looked up. "Have I?"

"You carry your father's silence now," she replied. "And your
eyes see things they didn't before."

Cael gave a small nod, gaze fixed on the fire. "The Institute has a way of doing that."

Stephen hesitated. "There's more to it than just the classes. The shadows… they feel alive there. Like they're waiting."

Cael's jaw tensed. "They always are."

The air thickened — not with fear, but with memory. Elara reached across the table and placed a hand over Stephen's. "The shadows aren't your enemy, Stephen. But they are never your servant either. Remember that."

"I do," he said. "Most of the time."

His father's eyes — a deep gray, flecked with ember — met his. "Then make sure you remember it when the light starts lying to you."

Stephen frowned faintly, unsure what he meant, but he nodded all the same.

Later that night, he couldn't sleep.

He stood outside, barefoot in the snow, the moon burning through the clouds. His breath came in thin, silver ribbons. The forest was silent — too silent. Every sound had sunk beneath the frost.

The mark beneath his wrist began to glow again, faintly silver. And for the first time, he saw something move through the trees — not a shadow exactly, but something *watching*.

He didn't speak. Didn't move.

Only when the wind shifted did he glimpse its eyes — silver, like his own, set in a shape that wasn't human. For an instant, he felt both terrified and seen.

Then it was gone.

When he returned inside, his mother was waiting in the hallway, candle in hand. "Stephen?"
He froze. "I couldn't sleep."

She studied him for a moment — the snow on his feet, the pale sheen in his eyes — and then simply said, "Your father used to walk like that, too."

The night passed without further whispers.
But in his dreams, Stephen stood once again before the Veil — and it no longer looked like a barrier.

It looked like a door.

Chapter XXVII — Echoes in the Frost

Morning came softly to Duskford.
The snow still lay deep, blanketing the town in muted silence,
but sunlight filtered through the fog — pale, uncertain, and
trembling over rooftops.

Stephen woke to the scent of cedar smoke and tea. His mother
was already in the kitchen, humming faintly as she pressed
herbs into a pot. The faint rhythm of a hammer drifted in from
outside — his father was at the forge again, despite the cold.

For the first time since leaving Everveil, Stephen felt
something close to peace.

But beneath that calm, something *else* stirred — the faint ache
of the mark beneath his wrist, like a heartbeat out of sync with
his own.

He flexed his hand. The mark shimmered once, then faded.
The wolf — whatever it had been — had not returned.

He hoped that meant it was content.

By midday, the snow had lightened enough for him to walk
into the town square. Duskford was alive again, if only faintly
— merchants sweeping porches clear of ice, children throwing
snowballs at the frozen fountain. It all felt impossibly normal.
Stephen almost forgot that just beyond the horizon, the
shadows still whispered.

"Stephen Umbra?"

The voice came from behind him — deep, weathered, and
oddly familiar. He turned.

A man in Veilguard gray stood near the old well, his coat dusted with frost. His face was half-hidden beneath a hood, but the insignia stitched to his shoulder gleamed unmistakably: the sigil of the **Cascade Division**.

"Yes," Stephen said cautiously.

The man smiled faintly, the kind that didn't quite reach the eyes. "Your father said I'd find you here."

"My father?" Stephen's heart kicked once, then steadied. "What for?"

The man gestured to the woods beyond the square. "Walk with me."

They followed the old path leading toward the edge of the forest. The air thickened the deeper they went, shadows curling between the trees like coiled ink.

"You've been marked," the man said at last. "The Institute's record confirms it."

Stephen's pulse quickened. "You know about that?"

"More than you'd think. The Veilguard keeps track of emerging bonds. When a familiar first begins to awaken, it tends to… ripple."

Stephen hesitated. "You're saying you felt it."

"I'm saying *everyone* in the Northwest did," the man replied. "Every shadowcaster worth their name felt the Veil stir three nights ago. Whatever tether you've formed—it's strong. Dangerous, maybe. But rare."

They stopped near a clearing where the snow had melted in a perfect circle.
The man crouched, running a gloved hand across the wet earth. "The Veil thins here too. Duskford sits on old ground. Watch yourself, Umbra. This isn't a safe place for an awakening."

Stephen frowned. "Then why tell me?"

"Because your father asked me to," he said simply. "And because when it comes, you'll want to be ready."

"When *what* comes?"

The man's gray eyes lifted toward him, glinting like iron. "The call."

Before Stephen could speak, the man vanished—his form unraveling into shadow, leaving behind nothing but footprints that filled slowly with snow.

That night, Stephen stood once more at his window, staring toward the tree line. The air was unnaturally still.

He thought of the man's words.
He thought of the mark.
He thought of the wolf.

The wind whispered through the forest, soft and strange.

And then, for just a moment, the world *shifted.*

The snow outside rippled like water. The shadows moved on their own.
And beyond the glass, Stephen saw the faintest glimmer of

eyes — not one pair this time, but many — watching from the forest's edge.

The Veil was stirring again.

Chapter XXVIII — Gifts of the Umbra

The last night in Duskford came wrapped in silence.
The snow had hardened into a glittering crust beneath the moon, and the air outside the Umbra home hung still and brittle, as if the world itself were holding its breath.

Inside, the hearth burned low — a single ember's glow reflecting across the family's oak table. Stephen sat between his parents, the warmth of the fire flickering across their faces.

Neither of them spoke for a while.
Then Cael broke the quiet.

"You've grown," his father said simply, his voice deep and edged with something between pride and concern. "And the Veil's eyes are turning your way now. That means we can no longer keep certain things from you."

Elara glanced toward the mantle, where an old wooden chest rested beneath the shadow of the family crest — the wolf and the crescent moon intertwined in silver thread.

"Your blood carries weight, Stephen," she said softly. "It's time you understood what that means."

Cael stood, crossing to the chest. He laid a broad hand atop it, and for a moment the carvings along its edges glimmered faintly with runes older than the Institute itself. With a quiet click, the chest opened.

Inside were two objects.
The first — a pendant of dark glass veined with silver, shaped like a drop of moonlight.
The second — a dagger wrapped in gray leather, its hilt engraved with shadow-script.

Cael lifted the dagger first, turning it so that the fire caught the faint etchings along its blade. "This belonged to the first Umbra who ever walked between the Veil," he said. "Forged from the obsidian of the Shadow Rift itself. It's called *Veyr's Fang*."

Stephen reached for it, but his father shook his head.

"This weapon isn't for war," Cael continued. "It's for *binding*. It answers not to blood, but to truth. When drawn with purpose, it can seal or sever any shadow tether — familiar, oath, or curse. It will weigh your intent. If you lie to it… it will know."

Slowly, he placed the dagger in Stephen's hands. The metal was cold — unnaturally so — and as his fingers curled around the hilt, a faint pulse passed through it, answering the mark on his wrist.

Elara stepped forward next, holding the pendant.

"This," she said, her voice quiet but steady, "is called the *Lumen Tear*. It was given to me by my grandmother, and to her by hers before. It channels the light hidden inside shadow. You'll understand that one day."

She lifted it gently, clasping it around Stephen's neck.
The silver light within flickered once — as though breathing.

"When the night feels endless," she whispered, "this will remind you that darkness was never meant to blind. Only to protect."

Stephen looked between them both — his mother's kind eyes, his father's proud stillness.
For a moment, the ache of leaving returned, sharp and familiar.

Cael rested a hand on his shoulder. "You'll leave for the train at first light," he said. "Your path's your own now. But remember, son — the shadows don't just hide monsters. They hide your strength, too."

That night, long after his parents had gone to bed, Stephen stood once more at his window. The pendant glowed faintly against his chest, its light reflecting across the blade of *Veyr's Fang* resting on his desk.

Beyond the glass, the wolf's silhouette flickered again — distant, patient, waiting in the forest mist.

For the first time, Stephen didn't flinch.

He raised the dagger slightly.
The runes along its edge pulsed in answer, whispering his name in a voice only the Veil could hear

UMBRA

Chapter XXIX — Shadows Return

The train to Everveil cut through a world locked in glass. Frost sheathed the trees, and the rails hissed as silver steam spilled into the morning air. Stephen sat by the window, the *Lumen Tear* cool against his chest, its faint pulse steady like a second heartbeat.

He turned the pendant once between his fingers. Every so often, the veins of silver inside it caught the passing light — and for a breath, the reflection looked like a wolf's eye staring back at him.

Kael Thane — always the first to break a silence — leaned across the aisle.
"Still staring into the void?" he asked, smirking. "You'll freeze your soul doing that."

Stephen smiled faintly. "Better than listening to you snore."

Kael's grin widened. "That's Veilguard-grade snoring, I'll have you know."

They both laughed quietly. Outside, the shadowed outline of the Cascades loomed closer — jagged and dark beneath a white sky.

It was the first day of January. In three days, the Institute would resume classes.

When the train crested the ridge, Everveil came into view once more — towers of black stone rising from the mist, windows glowing faintly in the morning haze. The massive ring sigil that crowned the gate shimmered with restrained light, tracing the seven Houses in silent order.

The moment Stephen stepped through the gates, the world seemed to *listen.*
The shadows rippled at his feet — and then vanished, as if retreating into the stone.

He swallowed hard. The pendant warmed against his skin.

Inside the Great Hall, the familiar hum of returning students filled the air. Banners of the seven Houses hung high above: the crescent moon of Shadows, the blazing phoenix of Flame, the mountain of Stone, the spiral wave of Tides, the storm-ring, the radiant sun, and the silver eye of Mind.

At the high table stood Headmistress Veyra and the seven Archons — one for each House. She raised a hand for silence.

"Students of Everveil," she said, her voice like wind through frost, "welcome back to the second term. The Solstice has passed, and the shadows grow restless once more. This year will test you. Some will falter. Some will rise. All will change."

The banners flickered — each sigil glowing once in silent acknowledgment.

Kael leaned toward Stephen and whispered, "That's her version of 'welcome back.' Warm as ever."

Stephen almost smiled.
Almost.

Classes resumed quickly. Days blurred between spell forms, incantations, and shadow theory. But beneath it all, something else stirred — a current unseen.

Late one evening, Stephen returned to his dorm. The fire had gone out, and the room was swallowed by dim gray light from the moon. On his desk lay a folded note written in a thin, elegant script.

"The Veil is stirring again. Watch the mirrors. —V."

He froze.
The pendant flared softly in answer.

Before he could react, Kael stepped in, shaking the snow from his coat. "You look like you saw a ghost," he said, then paused. "Wait—don't tell me you *did*."

Stephen handed him the note silently.

Kael frowned. "V? That's not a name, that's a threat."

Stephen's eyes lingered on the window, where frost traced strange circular patterns — not random, not natural. *Runes.*

"Maybe," he murmured, "it's both."

That night, long after Kael fell asleep, Stephen lay awake. The pendant pulsed against his chest. The dagger beneath his pillow whispered faintly — too faint to understand, but enough to know it was waiting.

Outside, the moon broke through the clouds, and from somewhere deep within the Veil, something whispered back.

"Soon."

"Soon."

Chapter XXX — The Final Shadow (Epilogue)

Far from the quiet light of Everveil, the storm broke over a land unremembered.

The fortress of Malrec lay in ruin—black towers shattered and smoking, the air still alive with whispers that had no mouth to speak them. Yet deep beneath that ruin, where the earth met shadow, something stirred.

A single figure stood among the broken stones: a man cloaked in the remnants of night itself. His hands bled from carving runes into the altar before him, the words forming a circle that pulsed with faint, rhythmic life.

Malrec's sigils had not died with him. They had *changed.*

"The heir has taken his name," the man said quietly, voice carrying through the ruined hall like the breath of the Veil itself. "And the moon burns again above the Cascades."

He looked up.

The sky was split.

A thin wound had opened above the mountains—a seam of light and shadow intertwined, trembling as if holding back a tide. From within it, faint echoes of screams drifted—ancient, forgotten, yet terrifyingly familiar.

"The world has named its champions," the man whispered. "Now it will name its judge."

He reached out toward the rippling light. The shadows bent to his touch, twisting around his fingers like serpents. The mark of the Veil flared to life on his palm—a brand of shifting black that refused to stay still.

The man smiled. Not in joy, but in remembrance.

"Veritas in Tenebris," he murmured—the ancient vow of the Umbra bloodline.
Then he turned toward the north, where the light of Everveil flickered faintly across the horizon.

"Let them find their truth," he said. "And let the darkness find its heir."

As he vanished into the mists, the wound in the sky widened.
The stars dimmed, one by one.
And the world began to forget that dawn had ever truly existed.

Chapter XXXI — The Hollow Name

The rain returned before dawn.

By the time Stephen stepped from the carriage at the gates of
Everveil, the sky had already surrendered to the storm — a
low, silver-black pall that rolled across the Cascades and
swallowed the light. Snow clung to the treetops, but it was the
kind that melted before it reached the ground, dissolving into
mist. Everything smelled of wet pine and iron.

He drew his coat tighter and looked back toward the forest
road. The lamps of Duskford shimmered faintly through the
fog, already fading into memory. The holidays had passed too
quickly — a blur of firelight, quiet laughter, and the scent of
his mother's winter tea. He still wore the obsidian pendant
she'd given him; its cool weight rested against his chest like a
promise.

The gates creaked open.

Kael waited just beyond them, snow in his dark hair, a
crooked smile breaking the cold.
"You made it," he said. "They were about to start without
you."

"Start what?" Stephen asked, stepping inside.

"The Headmistress's assembly. New term. New assignments.
Same lecture about restraint."
Kael rolled his eyes. "And apparently, something new on the
mission board."

They passed through the archway and into Everveil's
courtyard. The banners of the Seven Houses rippled overhead,
heavy with meltwater — obsidian, gold, and indigo catching
what little light broke through the clouds. The House of

Shadows' banner hung nearest the central tower, its crescent moon and wolf sigil gleaming faintly under the rain.

Inside the Grand Hall, warmth and candlelight battled the storm. Students filled the rows of benches, their chatter low and restless. At the far end, Headmistress Veyra stood beneath the carved seal of Everveil — seven sigils encircling the moon. Her voice carried easily over the murmurs.

"Balance," she was saying, "is not merely the art of restraint. It is the art of understanding the darkness you carry. Only by facing it can you wield it."

Stephen listened, but his mind wandered.
The shadows near the pillars seemed to breathe.

When the assembly ended, Professor Alren — tall, silver-eyed, and always half-absent — intercepted them near the corridor. "Mr. Umbra," he said, voice soft but edged. "You'll attend Shadowcraft Theory with me this term. We begin tomorrow."

Stephen nodded. "Yes, Professor."

As Alren turned to leave, his tone changed — quieter, almost to himself.
"The world remembers its mistakes," he murmured. "Even when the Veil tries to forget them."

Kael frowned. "What was that?"

But Alren was already gone.

Later that night

Snow whispered against the glass as Stephen sat at his desk. The candle beside him trembled, its flame bowing toward the window. He had meant to write home, but the page before him remained blank.

His pendant pulsed once, faintly.

The sound reached him then — a low hum, almost imperceptible, threading through the quiet. It came from the corridor beyond his door. He rose, barefoot, and stepped into the hall. The air smelled of dust and stone, though the torches burned steady.

At the far end, something shimmered across the wall — not a reflection, but a distortion, as though the stones themselves were remembering light. And carved into one of them, nearly hidden beneath centuries of soot, was a sigil.

A crescent enclosed within an open circle.
The mark throbbed with dim violet light.

When he reached for it, the flame in the nearest torch went out.

For an instant, he saw a figure standing beside him — a silhouette made of absence. Eyes like pale glass. And then it was gone, leaving only the whisper of his own breath and a voice, faint and wrong, curling through the air:

"Malrec."

His tattoo burned beneath his sleeve.

Stephen stumbled back, clutching his wrist as the pain faded. The light in the corridor flickered back to normal. But the name lingered, woven through the dark like an echo too old to die.

Chapter XXXII — The Whisper in the Glass

The snow deepened as the week passed.
By the third morning of Winter Term, Everveil was a
cathedral of white and shadow. The courtyard fountains had
frozen solid; the trees along the north wall bowed under a
weight of ice. Every sound — footsteps, laughter, even the
ringing of the bells — seemed muted, swallowed by the cold.

Stephen hadn't told anyone about the sigil. Not Kael, not even
Professor Alren. He had spent each night since staring at his
wrist, half-expecting the faint burn to return. It didn't. But
sometimes, when the lights dimmed and silence took the halls,
he could feel the stone beneath his dormitory hum softly, as
though the Veil itself were breathing.

In Shadowcraft Theory, Alren spoke of resonance — of the
way every shadow carried an echo of its origin.
"Darkness," he said, pacing before the dim class, "is memory
unclaimed. It does not vanish; it waits. To wield it, one must
listen before commanding."

Stephen tried. But what he heard that day was not memory. It
was something else.

The Hall of Mirrors

After lessons, Kael caught up with him near the archway that
led to the lower wings.
"House of Shadows patrol tonight," he said. "Professor Soren
wants us checking the Mirror Hall. Some lights flickering on
their own again."

Stephen frowned. "The mirrors under the west wing? I thought they were sealed."

Kael shrugged. "So did everyone else."

They descended together, the air growing colder with every step. The torches thinned until only their lanterns cast light. When they reached the Hall of Mirrors, frost filmed the glass in each pane — hundreds of tall, arched mirrors lining both walls like a thousand waiting eyes.

Their reflections swayed faintly, though neither of them moved.

Kael muttered, "That's not normal."

Stephen stepped closer to one of the mirrors. Beneath the frost, faint shapes stirred — not his face, but something older, deeper. The reflection smiled when he didn't. Its eyes were pale silver, its mouth a hollow curve.

Then it whispered a word he couldn't understand. The glass shivered like a heartbeat.

Kael grabbed his shoulder. "Did you hear that?"

Before Stephen could answer, the mirror directly across from them exploded outward. Shards spiraled through the air, yet not one touched them. The fragments hung there, suspended, forming a slow circle — and at its center appeared a mark.

The same sigil from the corridor.

Crescent and circle.
The mark of Malrec.

A pulse of violet light rolled down the hall, extinguishing the torches one by one until only their lanterns glowed weakly. Stephen's mark flared on his arm, bright and searing, before dimming again.

The fragments fell. Silence returned.

Kael breathed hard, lowering his hand. "What the hell was that?"

Stephen stared at the place where the sigil had burned against the wall. "A warning," he said softly.
He didn't know why he believed it. He just did.

Aftermath

They filed a report with Professor Soren. The mirrors were sealed again by morning, covered with veils of iron-threaded cloth. No one spoke of the incident openly, though whispers spread among the upper years — tales of curses, of a presence moving through the halls unseen.

Stephen lay awake that night, watching moonlight drift through the window and scatter across his desk. It gleamed faintly on the black pendant his mother had given him. For an instant, the reflection on its surface wasn't his own.

It was the same hollow smile he'd seen in the mirror.

The whisper returned, soft as breath against glass.

"Malrec."

Chapter XXXIII — The Shadow Between Bells

Morning light bled weakly through the frost-coated windows of Everveil. The sky had turned from gray to white, snow falling in slow, endless spirals. Bells tolled for morning assembly — deep, solemn, and cold as iron.

Stephen sat at the long table in the refectory, pushing a half-eaten plate of bread aside. The conversation around him blurred into background noise: students laughing, spells flickering between hands, the crackle of firelight in the central hearth. But his mind kept drifting back to the whisper.

"Malrec."

The sound had embedded itself in his skull like a song half-remembered.

Across from him, Kael leaned back in his chair. "You haven't slept."

"Not much."

Kael tore a piece of bread and shrugged. "You're thinking about the mirror."

Stephen looked up. "It wasn't just a haunting, Kael. That mark—it reacted to me."

Kael's eyes narrowed slightly. "Or you reacted to it."

Neither spoke for a while. The fire cracked. Then, faintly, a sound from beyond the hall—like a string being plucked—echoed through the air.

The bells began to toll again, but out of rhythm this time. Too fast. Too sharp. Students fell silent, glancing upward as the final bell rang once and shattered into a hundred silver fragments midair.

Screams followed.

The Distortion

Headmistress Veyra entered almost instantly, her cloak trailing lines of shadow that reformed into her boots as she crossed the threshold.
"Stay calm!" her voice rang. "The Veil trembles, but it is not breaking."

The words did little to settle the rising panic. The windows darkened; frost thickened until even candlelight bent through it in warped streaks. Stephen could see his reflection in the frost — but the reflection wasn't his. It was grinning.

He felt the amulet at his chest pulse once. Then again.

Kael grabbed his arm. "Stephen. Look."

Up near the high beams of the ceiling, black feathers began to drift down — not ash, not snow, but feathers made of mist. When they touched the floor, they melted into shadow. And with them came a faint voice that everyone could hear but no one could locate.

"Everveil," it whispered. "Your debt approaches."

The headmistress lifted a hand, drawing a sigil in the air with glowing ink of gold and silver. The mark flared, sealing the ceiling shut with layered wards. The distortion quieted.

But Stephen still heard it—soft, low, and near.

Your mark… it listens.

The Headmistress's Office

Later that day, Stephen and Kael were summoned to the headmistress's office. The walk there felt heavier than before. The corridor torches dimmed when they passed, as if wary.

Headmistress Veyra stood before a high, narrow window overlooking the snow-covered valley. Her expression was unreadable.

"You saw the sigil," she said without turning.

Stephen nodded. "Yes. It—spoke."

"And it spoke *his* name," Veyra said, her tone quiet but edged. "Malrec. I had hoped it was myth, but myths have a way of finding their believers."

Kael frowned. "Who is he, really?"

Veyra turned then, her eyes like silvered glass. "A heretic of the old Veil Orders. A shadowmancer who sought to pierce the border between worlds. When he failed, he was consumed. But legends say he left his mark behind—waiting for a vessel strong enough to bear it."

Stephen felt the air thicken. "A vessel…"

"Perhaps it found one," Veyra said softly, watching him.

He lowered his gaze. "If that's true, then tell me how to stop it."

The headmistress hesitated, then reached into her sleeve and pulled out a small obsidian ring carved with faint runes. "This was once used to seal echoes within the Veil," she said. "Wear it while you sleep. If the voice calls, listen—but do not answer."

Stephen took it carefully. The metal was cold enough to sting.

As he and Kael left, the snow outside began to fall harder, the flakes turning gray as they touched the ground.

Somewhere beyond the forest, a bell that no one had rung tolled once more.

Chapter XXXIV — Shadows in Motion

Snow blanketed Everveil in silence. The training yard was a cathedral of frost and breath, every sound swallowed by the falling cold. Students of the House of Shadows moved through drills beneath the dim blue lanterns that lined the perimeter — each swing, step, and word part of an ancient cadence meant to bind magic to motion.

At the center stood Stephen and Kael, facing each other across a ring of chalk and ash.

"Again," called Instructor Veyra's lieutenant, Master Corin, his voice sharp as flint. "Control, not power!"

Stephen raised his hand. The shadow beneath his feet rippled outward like spilled ink, reaching for Kael. Kael countered with a flick of his wrist, the air around him shivering as light condensed into thin lines. The shadows shattered against them like glass.

Corin nodded. "Better. But again."

They'd been at it for hours.

The Weight of Focus

When the lesson finally ended, steam rose from the two of them as they leaned against the courtyard's stone wall. The air smelled faintly of salt and iron.

Kael exhaled hard. "She's trying to kill us."

Stephen smirked. "If she wanted us dead, she'd stop correcting your stance."

Kael threw a snowball at him. "You wish."

But beneath the teasing, both could feel it — the pressure building, the awareness that this wasn't ordinary training. Everveil's upper instructors had doubled the House of Shadows' regimen since the bell's destruction. Every sigil, every spell, every mental exercise was tuned toward one purpose: containment.

That night, Stephen sat on his bed in the dormitory, the obsidian ring on his finger catching the firelight. The mark beneath his shirt pulsed faintly — almost in rhythm with the wind outside.

When he closed his eyes, the world behind them wasn't his own.

The Dream of Mirrors

He stood in a corridor of mirrors — cracked, shifting, endless. His reflection moved a heartbeat too late. In each reflection, his eyes glowed differently: blue, silver, black.

Then a voice came. Smooth. Amused. Ancient.

"Learning control?"

He turned — but there was no one there. Only another mirror, showing him older, colder, and cloaked in shadow.

"Power isn't about restraint," the reflection whispered. *"It's about knowing when to stop pretending."*

Stephen reached toward it — and woke up gasping.

Kael stirred in the bed across the room. "Another nightmare?"

Stephen nodded, wiping sweat from his brow. "Not mine. I think he's trying to talk to me."

Kael sat up. "Then we'll make sure he never gets the chance."

The Next Morning

Classes resumed with a new rhythm. Combat drills turned brutal. Meditation exercises stretched hours past curfew. For those in the House of Shadows, failure was no longer marked by a score — it was marked by silence, the kind that followed a student collapsing under exhaustion.

Still, something within Stephen had sharpened. His control improved. The mark at his chest no longer burned; it *waited.*

When Headmistress Veyra called an assembly at dusk, the air hummed with expectation. She stood at the dais, flanked by the banners of all seven Houses.

"The Mission Board reopens tomorrow," she announced. "Second-years and above may apply for sanctioned operations beyond the walls. Choose carefully — the Veil's fractures are growing."

Kael looked at Stephen, a grin tugging at his lips. "Guess we're about to see what all that control was for."

Stephen smiled faintly, though his gaze lingered on the banners swaying in the lanternlight.

Something told him control might not be enough.

Chapter XXXV — The Cavern of Hollow Stars

The wind cut sharp through the stone corridors of Everveil's outer training grounds, scattering frost and whispers alike. The mission board shimmered faintly under torchlight, its runes alive with unseen intent — a soft hum that only those tied to the Veil could truly hear.

Stephen paused in front of it, the paper edges flickering like something breathing. The crowd of students behind him murmured about easy patrols and low-tier retrievals, but the shadows around the board were shifting differently tonight — deeper, alive, watchful.

Kael came up beside him, his breath a pale fog in the cold. "You feel that too, right?"

Stephen nodded slowly. "The board's choosing."

A ripple spread across the parchment — and then, ink bled outward, rewriting one of the listings.

Cave system north of the Cascades.
Uncharted. Origin unknown.
Objective: Exploration and artifact retrieval.
Reward: Rights to all recovered spoils.

Kael gave a low whistle. "That's not on the public registry."

Stephen's eyes narrowed. "Then it's meant for us."

The runes flared in agreement — shadows coiling up their arms in fine black filaments that dissolved as quickly as they appeared. A silent seal of choice.

By dusk, the two were already descending the frozen mountain paths north of Everveil. The moon was fractured above them, its light threading through mist and pine like broken glass. Their boots crunched on old snow as the path narrowed into a canyon that bled darkness from its walls.

Kael adjusted his satchel, glancing toward the valley below. "You realize this is how all the bad stories start, right? Two idiots chasing a whisper into a cave?"

Stephen smirked faintly. "Then let's make sure it ends differently."

The cavern mouth yawned like a wound in the mountain. Frost clung to the stalactites, glittering with veins of faint blue light — not natural, not ordinary. Deeper still, the air grew warm, humming with a low frequency that vibrated in their bones.

They hadn't gone far before they heard movement ahead — deliberate, light, not echoing quite right.

A familiar voice drifted from the dark. "You two again? You really do have a habit of finding trouble."

Kael tensed — then relaxed with a half-smile. "Arienna Valeith. I should've guessed."

Two figures stepped into the lanternlight — Arienna with her ember-copper hair pulled into a braid, and Soren Corren beside her, expression unreadable as always. The faint silver reflection of his eyes caught the light like mirrors.

Stephen nodded slightly. "Didn't expect to see you outside the library archives again."

Arienna smirked. "We go where the work is. And right now, this cave is our assignment."

Soren tilted his head, assessing the two. "Or perhaps it's both of ours. The Veil tends to overlap… intentionally."

Before Stephen could reply, the ground shuddered beneath their feet.

A screech tore through the darkness — piercing, ancient. The air rippled with heat and light as something massive lunged from the depths.

A creature of half-stone, half-flesh, its body threaded with crystal veins and molten eyes — a **crag wyrm**, rare and furious, followed by two smaller, pale beasts that moved like liquid shadow.

"Back!" Stephen shouted.

The group scattered as the wyrm's tail slammed into the ground, spraying shards of glowing rock. Kael rolled to his feet, conjuring a flare of white light that blinded one of the shadow beasts long enough for Stephen's blade to find it.

Arienna raised her hands, fire licking across her palms — her blast collided with the wyrm's flank, searing through the crystal, but it only enraged the beast further. Soren's eyes gleamed silver as he cast a web of reflective illusions, splitting their images into a dozen ghostly copies across the cavern walls.

Kael darted through one of them, driving his blade deep into the wyrm's throat — just enough to make it stagger. Stephen surged forward, channeling his shadow energy through his weapon.

The darkness sang as steel met stone, a shockwave rippling outward.

When the echoes faded, the cavern was silent except for their breathing. The wyrm's carcass lay still, its molten veins cooling to dull amber.

Kael leaned against the wall, panting. "Well… that was educational."

Soren was already kneeling beside the corpse, prying loose shards of crystal with an alchemist's precision. "These cores are Veil-reactive. If we forge them into armor, they'll channel energy — not block it."

Arienna grinned. "Guess we're keeping the spoils, then."

Stephen nodded, examining the faint black residue the shadow creatures had left behind. "We'll take what we can use. But we camp here tonight. The Veil's thick — it'll be safer if we stay together."

They cleared a space near the cavern's entrance. Kael kindled a small flame, Arienna reinforcing it with her heat until it burned steady and golden. Shadows played on the walls, their movements slower now — almost peaceful.

Soren sat cross-legged, working the crystal shards into small, rough shapes. "Not bad for a team that keeps running into each other by accident."

Kael chuckled. "Accident? Feels like the Veil's got a sense of humor."

Stephen smiled faintly, his gaze tracing the flickering firelight. "Or maybe it's trying to tell us something."

Outside, the wind howled through the mountains, carrying with it whispers that none of them noticed — words older than language itself.
The kind that watched.
The kind that remembered

Chapter XXXVI — The Hall of the Ebon Vow

The torches guttered low as the four descended deeper into the mountain, the air thick with dust and the scent of age. Shadows pressed against the cavern walls, pulsing faintly as if alive. They had been walking for hours — further and further into a network of twisting tunnels that seemed to breathe.

Soren ran his hand along the wall, tracing faint carvings. "This stone isn't natural. Someone shaped this place long ago."

Arienna's flame-glow illuminated faded reliefs of hooded figures and beasts locked in battle. "Then whoever did it wanted to keep it hidden."

Stephen felt it too — the low hum beneath the rock, old power calling to his blood. Every step down the spiral path seemed to echo louder, the sound of four heartbeats blending with something older.

The tunnels widened abruptly into a vast hollow chamber.

The walls glimmered faintly with veins of violet crystal. Ruined columns jutted from the floor like broken ribs, and scattered bones and armor fragments hinted at countless failed expeditions.

"Looks like we're not the first ones here," Kael muttered, drawing his blade.

They barely had time to react before the darkness *moved*.

Dozens of small, twisted creatures erupted from the ground — malformed shadows with jagged limbs and mouths like torn cloth. They screamed in unison, a chorus of despair that shook the air.

Arienna loosed a flare of fire, sending the front ranks reeling. Kael countered with a blast of spectral light that shattered two at once. Soren's mirrored illusions split across the cavern, confusing the horde, while Stephen cut through them in silent precision — shadows curling around his blade like smoke.

Even working together, the assault seemed endless. For every creature they struck down, two more rose from the fissures.

Then came the tremor.

A roar like thunder split the air as a colossal creature emerged from the far side of the cavern — a nightmare formed of bone and molten stone, six-limbed, with an eye of ember fire in the center of its chest.

"The guardian," Soren hissed.

It lunged, claws tearing through rock. Stephen dodged, rolling to the side as the ground exploded beneath him. Kael raised both hands, chanting low; veins of cold necrotic blue ran across his skin as he summoned a barrier of spectral bone that cracked under the beast's strike.

Arienna's arrows streaked through the gloom, igniting as they flew — but each impact barely slowed the creature. It caught one midair and *crushed* it in its hand, fire snuffing out.

Soren appeared behind it, slashing with twin illusory blades that shattered its back armor — but the blow nearly threw him against the wall.

"We're not going to kill it fighting separately!" Stephen shouted.

Kael met his eyes, nodding once. "Then together."

They moved as one.

Arienna lit the chamber in fire; Soren's mirrors amplified it into a prism of blinding radiance. Kael's necrotic sigils spread across the floor, anchoring the creature's limbs with spectral chains, while Stephen drove forward — his shadow wrapping his sword in a storm of obsidian flame.

The creature roared one last time as the blade struck its heart.

For a moment, there was only silence — then the guardian crumbled to ash, its molten eye fading to a single spark that drifted down and vanished.

They stood among the ruin, breathless.

"Remind me," Kael said, wiping sweat from his brow, "to never follow you into a cave again."

Arienna chuckled weakly. "You say that every time."

They began to scavenge — crystal shards, scraps of relic metal, fragments of obsidian armor that pulsed faintly with Veillight. It was Soren who found it — half-buried behind the guardian's corpse.

A wall carved with a symbol.

The **Umbra crest.**

The wolf and crescent glowed faintly beneath layers of dust.

"Stephen," Soren murmured.

Stephen approached slowly, his pulse matching the hum in the air. He reached out — and the moment his fingertips brushed the carving, the stone *shifted.*

A low groan rolled through the cavern as the crest flared with blue fire and split down the middle, revealing a stairway descending into a dark beyond.

The steps led downward for what felt like forever. Each wall was engraved with scenes of shadow and light, battles between figures crowned with flame and shrouded in night.

When they reached the bottom, the air changed — colder, stiller, heavy with reverence.

They entered a vast circular chamber illuminated by hovering orbs of pale light. At the center stood an altar carved from black crystal, inscribed with seven ancient runes.

Around it, seven pedestals held weapons, each unlike the other — and seven chest plates forged of living metal, dark as oil and marked with animal sigils.

The moment they stepped forward, the air thickened, pressing on their chests. The orbs brightened — and faint voices whispered through the chamber.

**"We see you, heirs of shadow.
We know your names.
You were written before the Veil was sealed."**

Stephen's eyes widened. He could feel the energy wrapping around him — testing, judging, recognizing. His hand trembled as he reached toward the altar.

The weapon before him shimmered — a long sword of blackened steel with the Umbra motto etched in silver fire: *Veritas in Umbra.*

The blade pulsed once — then *merged* with the dagger at his hip, becoming one. The fusion was seamless. The weapon hummed like a heartbeat in sync with his own.

Kael stepped next. A tall necromantic staff of black bone and blue light leapt from its pedestal, spiraling around his arm before solidifying in his grip.

Arienna approached an obsidian bow — its limbs curved like wings of flame, veins of red energy glowing faintly. The weapon responded instantly to her presence, flaring bright as she touched it.

Soren's daggers shimmered and split into twin blades, one silver, one black, connected by fine threads of mirrored light.

Three relics remained: metal knuckle covers, a second staff, and a pair of plain black whips that seemed dormant.

"They're waiting," Kael murmured, "for the others who haven't come yet."

Suddenly, the air shifted again. The symbols above each of the chosen flared, sending streams of shadowlight curling across their arms.

Marks burned into their skin — intricate sigils of ancient design.

Stephen gasped as the mark on his forearm pulsed, spreading like liquid silver into the shape of a wolf's head intertwined with a crescent. His familiar's spirit shimmered faintly behind him, echoing the mark before fading into his skin.

Kael's sigil resembled a raven's outstretched wings.
Arienna's, a drake of living flame.
Soren's remained faint, mirrored lines forming an unblinking eye.

The armor shimmered, the chest plates melting into shadow and reforming around them — light, seamless, alive. When they willed it, it vanished; when called, it returned in an instant.

The altar pulsed once more. A script unfurled across its surface in old Umbric — the language of the Veil.

**"Seven shall rise when the moon is cleaved.
Bound by vow, chosen by shadow,
They will walk between realms
Until the heir awakens and the Veil is broken.
On his eighteenth dawn,
The gates shall open once more."**

Kael exhaled slowly. "Eighteen… that's three years from now."

Stephen's expression hardened. "Then that's the time we have left."

The lights dimmed. The chamber went still. But as they turned to leave, the runes above the altar ignited again, branding their names into the stone — in the language of prophecy.

EBON VOW.
Umbra. Thane. Valeith. Corren.

And below them — three empty spaces.

Waiting.

Chapter XXXVII — The Oaths Beneath the Mountain (Canon-Perfect Version)

The fire crackled low against the mouth of the cave, its smoke curling into the frozen night. Beyond, the wind sighed through the pines — but inside, a stillness lingered, thick with the echo of something ancient.

Four figures sat around the flame. Their armor still shimmered faintly with Veillight — living metal etched with sigils that pulsed in rhythm with their hearts. The air hummed softly between them, alive with new magic.

Between them lay the spoils of their descent: blackened coins, shards of crystal, chunks of creature bone and ore that whispered of shadowfire.

Lunaris laid the last relic down and leaned back, his blade — the one the Veil itself had forged to replace his dagger — resting across his knees.

The shadows stirred.

At first, they moved subtly, like ink spreading through water. Then, one by one, the relics and materials slid into place — separating into four equal piles. Even the scattered gold divided neatly, aligning with precision beyond mortal intent.

Nyx watched, eyes wide. "It's splitting them evenly…"

Veyr gave a short laugh, dry and awed. "Guess even shadows like fairness."

Lunaris shook his head, gaze fixed on the movement. "Not fairness. Balance. The Vow's first answer."

When the division ended, three relics remained untouched: the metal knuckle guards, the spare staff, and the coiled whips. They pulsed faintly — not inert, but waiting.

Corvus nodded toward them. "Then they're for the others. When they come."

"Then we keep them safe," Lunaris said, wrapping them carefully in dark cloth. "Until the seven are whole."

The silence that followed wasn't empty.
It was full — heavy with new breath, with understanding.

Nyx sat cross-legged beside the fire, tracing the faint ember-line of her familiar's sigil across her palm. A flicker of smoke curled up from her skin and dissipated. "It listens now. When I call."

Veyr leaned back, flipping one dagger through his fingers. Its edge caught the light and vanished again. "It's not just a weapon. It's a bond."

Corvus nodded slowly. "A covenant, then. We've accepted it. But it's accepted us, too."

Lunaris rose, his cloak shifting like liquid night. "Then we seal it properly."

He drove his blade into the ground — the steel ringing once, echoing deeper than sound. The shadows rippled outward, forming a circle that touched each of them. The fire dimmed until only the glow of their marks remained.

"The first vow," Lunaris said, his voice steady but solemn. "To bring the others here when they are chosen. To guide them to the relics. To never let this place — or what it means — be forgotten."

Corvus raised his staff. "We swear it."

"The second vow," Lunaris continued. "To protect the innocent. To never raise our blades against one another — or the families that gave us breath.
From this moment on, we are not just students. We are bound — one family, one Vow."

The shadows rose — slow, deliberate — weaving around their hands and blades. The mark of the Ebon Vow shimmered across each of their wrists, faint but eternal.

Nyx's voice came soft but firm. "One family."

Veyr joined, his tone quiet but certain. "The Ebon Vow."

Corvus closed his eyes, his words like a benediction. "Bound by shadow. Tempered by truth."

The shadows pulsed once, as if exhaling. The fire reignited, steady and calm.

Hours later, when the cave fell to silence, they settled near the embers.
Nyx slept first, her bow resting across her chest. Veyr kept watch, his mirrored daggers flickering with faint light at the cave's edge.

Corvus sat with his staff across his lap, whispering to the quiet.

Lunaris remained awake the longest, his sword beside him, eyes reflecting both fire and moonlight. He could still feel the circle's weight — not as a burden, but as something binding him to purpose.

He looked toward the cave mouth, where the wind whispered faintly against the dark.

The prophecy had begun.
The Ebon Vow was born.
And the Veil had found its chosen.

Chapter XXXVIII — The Forger of Market Street

The morning after their vows, the Ebon Vow descended from the mountains under a pale, fractured dawn. The mist clung to their cloaks and armor as if reluctant to release them, whispering through the trees like the remnants of the prophecy itself.

By noon, they reached Market Street — the lower ward of Everveil's outer town, where smoke and metal ruled the air. The place was alive with the clamor of the mundane and the magical. Steam hissed from vents beneath cobblestones; runes flickered faintly on every sign. Here, artisans forged both weapons and illusions. And at the end of the lane, beneath an arch of shadowed ivy, stood **The Forger**.

The door to his shop bore no name — only a sigil, burned deep into the black oak: a hammer striking a crescent moon. It pulsed once when they approached, recognizing them.

Lunaris pushed the door open.

The air inside was thick with heat and the scent of molten silver. Shadows bent unnaturally across the room, moving in rhythm with the pulse of the forge. At the far end, surrounded by sparks and smoke, stood an old man — broad-shouldered, eyes like dying embers.

"So," he said, without looking up, "the Vow returns from beneath the mountain."

Corvus blinked. "You knew we were coming?"

The Forger's mouth twitched, almost a smile. "The Veil always tells me when something new has been born."

He turned, and for the first time they saw that his right arm was made of iron — engraved with symbols that glowed faintly when he moved.
On the table before him were relic fragments, bones of beasts, and a pile of black-veined ore that looked disturbingly alive.

The Bargain

Lunaris stepped forward and unrolled a cloth bundle — the scavenged materials they'd collected from the cave. The Forger's gaze sharpened immediately.

"Good harvest," he said. "Shadowsteel veins. Boneglass. Aether scales. You've been busy."

Veyr smirked faintly. "Busy nearly dying."

Nyx stepped closer to the forge, her eyes reflecting the firelight. "We need these shaped. Armor, reinforced gear. Things that move with us."

The Forger's eyes flicked up, meeting hers — and then lingering on the faint glow of her vow mark. "Not *for* you," he said. "*With* you. The shadows don't answer to borrowed steel anymore. You'll forge them through your bond."

Corvus frowned. "You mean—"

"I mean," the Forger interrupted, "each of you will bleed into your creation."

He drew a thin, curved knife from his belt and set it on the anvil between them. "Shadowforging," he said. "Old magic. Costs nothing but pain and permanence."

The Forging

One by one, they stepped forward.

Lunaris first — placing his hand on the anvil, slicing the blade across his palm. His blood hissed as it struck the molten steel, turning the forge's flame silver-white. His sword pulsed in answer.

Corvus followed, his drop of blood flaring deep blue. The air filled with the sound of faint whispering — voices of the dead, swirling through the forge.

Nyx's blood burned orange, the flame dancing higher, her familiar's shadow rippling faintly behind her.

Veyr's was last — a streak of deep violet that froze the air around him, the metal hissing with frost and echo.

The Forger's hammer struck once for each of them, and the forge responded like a heartbeat.

When it was done, he quenched the glowing steel in a basin of black water. Steam erupted, whispering their names.

"Four forged," he said softly. "Bound by blood and shadow. You'll find no smith in this world or the next who can undo what you've made today."

They each received their creations — reforged armor plates, lighter, stronger, whispering faintly when worn. The shadows along the seams moved like living threads.

"These will grow with you," the Forger said, his tone grave.
"Feed them, and they'll serve. Neglect them, and they'll turn
on you.
The Veil gives nothing without hunger."

He turned away, returning to the heat. "When the next three
arrive," he added, "tell them I'll be waiting. The forge
remembers every oath."

Outside, dusk had begun to fall — red-gold and soft across the
street.
The four stood silently for a moment, the weight of their new
gear settling around them.

Corvus finally broke the quiet. "Feels like the first real day of
something."

Lunaris looked toward the horizon where the mountains met
the mist.
"No," he said softly. "Feels like the last day of peace."

The shadows at their feet stirred — faint, alive, listening.

And in the distance, though none of them knew it yet, the
name *Malrec* crossed a dying man's lips for the first time in
centuries.

Chapter XXXIX — The Weight of Steel and Shadow

The snow outside Everveil fell soft and slow, catching the lamplight in drifting ribbons of silver. The city was quieter tonight — as if the Veil itself was holding its breath.

Inside the dormitory commons of the **House of Shadows**, the four newly bound members of the Ebon Vow sat around the crackling fire, their new armor and weapons resting nearby like sleeping beasts. Each relic glimmered faintly with its own pulse — not light exactly, but presence.

Lunaris stared at his reforged sword where it lay across his knees. The blade no longer looked like mortal steel; it seemed to swallow light, its faint crescent etch glowing when his thoughts darkened. His familiar's shadow — the outline of a wolf's head — flickered against the wall.

"They feel heavier now," Nyx murmured, tracing her finger along the curve of her obsidian bow.
"Not the weight of metal," Veyr said quietly, "but of purpose."

Corvus smirked. "Purpose has a nasty habit of cutting deeper than any blade."

They laughed softly, though none of them truly felt lighthearted. The vow they'd made the night before still burned beneath their skin, a subtle, constant reminder that something vast and ancient now bound them.

The Whisper in the Hall

A knock came at the door.
Three soft taps. Then silence.

Veyr stood first, hand brushing one of his twin daggers as he opened it.
No one was there. Only a folded piece of parchment lay on the floor, sealed with a sigil none of them recognized — a **black spiral ringed by ash**.

Lunaris picked it up and held it near the fire. The seal shimmered, and the parchment unfolded itself in his hand.

"To the Veilborn Four,
The shadows speak of your descent. The next gate waits beneath the cliffs of Duskwood. The relics have awakened —
now prove you can bear their hunger.
— The Watcher."*

Corvus frowned. "Watcher? That's new."

"The Veil's testing us," Nyx said. "It wants to see if the prophecy wasn't a mistake."

Lunaris nodded slowly. "Then we'll show it."

The Mission Chosen

The next morning, the **mission board** shimmered to life in the central hall of Everveil — a massive ring of carved obsidian veins that rearranged themselves each term. Hundreds of shadowcasters gathered to watch as the new missions flared into being.

Headmistress Veyra's voice echoed across the hall.

"Each mission carries weight. Choose carefully. The Veil marks those who take more than they can bear."

Most students hesitated before the glowing sigils, whispering over the safer postings — shadow-wolves near the ridge, missing relics in the old archives. But when Lunaris stepped forward, his relic mark burned faintly through his sleeve. The sigils shifted on their own, rearranging until one pulsed in front of him:

Mission 14 — Duskwood Caverns Reclamation.
"Reported unstable shadows. Lost artifacts. Reward by weight in silver and relic credit."

He looked back to the others. Corvus just grinned. "Guess the Veil picked for us again."

They signed their names — their shadow names — in ink that shimmered like starlight. The sigil dimmed, sealing their fate.

Preparation and Unease

By dusk, the four had stocked provisions and checked their gear. Their familiars — silent for now — lingered in the corners of their senses, restless.

As they left the gates, Lunaris glanced back at the towers of Everveil. Snow drifted across the spires like falling ash.

He thought of his parents — of the **Umbra crest** hanging over the hearth — and the way his mother's eyes had shimmered when she gave him the pendant. It pulsed faintly now, as though in warning.

"Feels different this time," Nyx said as they reached the ridge. "It should," Corvus muttered. "We're not just students anymore."

Veyr's tone was softer. "No… we're something the shadows haven't seen in centuries."

The path ahead led into Duskwood — where the Veil grew thin, where whispers crawled along the roots of the trees. And somewhere beneath those cliffs, something ancient waited — watching through the eyes of the dark.

DUSKWOOD
CAVERNS
RECLAMATION

DUSKWOOD
CAVERRNS
RECLAMATION

Chapter XL — Shadows Over Greyhaven

The wind cut colder the farther they traveled from Everveil, carrying the scent of frost and burning wood. The world beyond the wards felt heavier — older somehow — as if the ground itself remembered the wars waged long before magic had names.

By dusk, the trees of Duskwood thinned, giving way to the edge of a wide valley where faint torchlight flickered against the snow. The town below was small — stone walls, peaked roofs, and the faint glow of life.

But above it hung a wound in the sky.

It was not light or darkness — it was absence. The Veil there had split open like torn fabric, revealing a jagged chasm of living shadow. Wisps of spectral energy leaked through, spiraling down into the town like smoke.

And beneath it, chaos.

The Town in Peril

"Greyhaven," Veyr breathed, eyes wide. "It's on the old maps. The first Veilguard outpost this side of the range."

Before any of them could respond, the sound of screaming reached them. Then the unmistakable echo of claws against stone.

Lunaris drew his blade. "We move."

They descended the ridge fast, their relic armor flickering into existence with bursts of shadowlight. By the time they reached the outer road, the first of the creatures emerged — thin, twisted things of bone and black flame, their forms rippling like oil.

Corvus spun his staff once, the sigils along its haft igniting. "Guess the Veil wanted to greet us personally."

"Let's return the favor," Lunaris said, eyes burning silver.

The Battle of Greyhaven

They hit the town square like a storm.

Nyx loosed a volley of shadow-tipped arrows, each one trailing flame and silver ash. Veyr moved beside her — silent, lethal — his twin daggers carving through the monsters' tendrils before they could reach the villagers.

Lunaris and Corvus took the front, sword and staff meeting shadowbeast after shadowbeast. With each kill, Lunaris' tattoos glowed brighter — faint silver lines tracing along his arms, matching the mark of his wolf familiar.

One creature lunged, its body a mass of shrieking faces. Lunaris met it head-on, his blade bursting with crescent fire as he cut through it in one sweeping arc. The explosion of shadow threw him backward into the mud, breath knocked from his chest.

And then, above the roar, came the cry —

"Veilguard! To the breach!"

Figures in grey and white cloaks appeared through the smoke, moving with military precision. Their runed rifles flared, cutting down the remaining beasts with blasts of spectral fire. The air crackled with the smell of ozone and blood.

For a long moment, all was still. Only the sound of falling ash remained.

The Meeting of Light and Shadow

A woman stepped forward from the Veilguard ranks — tall, with short silver hair and eyes like dawn. Her uniform bore the insignia of a captain. She studied them — the dark armor, the relics, the glow of shadowlight around them.

"You're not students," she said quietly. "Not anymore."

Lunaris lowered his sword. "We're from Everveil Institute. The Veil chose us."

A faint smirk touched her lips. "Then it chose well."

They exchanged introductions. The woman's name was **Captain Selene Dravik**, commander of the Pacific Veilguard Division. Her tone carried the practiced calm of someone who had seen too much.

"The breach opened three days ago," she said. "We've held the line, but something's stirring inside. Bigger than the usual riftspawn."

Lunaris glanced up at the tear. It pulsed faintly now, as though listening.

"We're headed for Duskwood Caverns," he said. "Something there called us."

Selene's eyes narrowed, but she nodded. "Then you're walking straight into the wound. If you make it back…" She paused, meeting Lunaris' gaze.

"Tell Everveil that the Veil bleeds faster than it heals."

She saluted, the Veilguard behind her doing the same. For a moment — one rare, silent moment — light and shadow bowed to each other.

Into the Cavern

By dawn, the Ebon Vow reached the cliffs of Duskwood. The air shimmered faintly with shadow energy, and the snow beneath their feet was blackened, as if burned by starlight.

From their vantage point, they could see the entrance to the cavern — a jagged maw in the cliff face, half-hidden by mist.

Corvus crouched, scanning the path. "There," he said. "Two sentinels — Veilspawn husks. Still guarding the place."

Nyx nocked an arrow. "We take them quietly?"

Lunaris shook his head. "We take them efficiently. In and out. We're not here for glory — we're here for truth."

Veyr smirked faintly. "Says the boy chosen by a sword older than the Veil itself."

Lunaris gave him a look, but said nothing. His gaze was already fixed on the dark below.

The Ebon Vow moved as one, their relics whispering against
the silence.
The Veil stirred in answer, deep and patient — waiting.

And somewhere in the depths of the cavern,
Malrec opened his eyes.

Chapter XLI — Descent into the Hollow Veil

The path down into the caverns wound like a scar through the stone.
Cold air breathed from the depths, carrying whispers that made the torchlight flicker.

The Ebon Vow moved carefully — Lunaris leading, his blade faintly glowing with silver flame; Corvus behind him, runes along his staff pulsing in rhythm with the Veil's heartbeat. Nyx and Veyr followed, quiet and watchful, their shadows slipping ahead like scouts.

"Feels wrong," Nyx murmured. "Like the air's too still — waiting for something."

Veyr knelt beside a carved pillar half-buried in dust. Old sigils marked its surface, glowing faintly as his fingers brushed them.

"These runes are pre-Everveil. Ancient Veilguard markings — from before the Institute was founded."

Lunaris glanced back. "Then this isn't a natural rift."

Corvus's voice was low. "No. It was built."

The Echo of Malrec

The deeper they went, the more the shadows seemed to listen.
Their own reflections warped against the cavern walls — stretched, elongated, twisted by the Veil's pulse.

At one point, a voice echoed through the chamber — faint, hollow, and unmistakably human.

"Power is not what corrupts," it whispered. "It is the refusal to wield it."

The torches dimmed.
For a moment, all four froze.

Corvus's grip tightened on his staff. "You all heard that, right?"

Nyx's expression was unreadable. "That wasn't an echo."

A tremor rippled through the floor, dust falling from the ceiling. Lunaris raised his sword, the flame within it flaring like a heartbeat.

"Keep moving," he said quietly. "We're being watched."

The Hall of Chains

The tunnel opened suddenly into a vast chamber, its ceiling lost in darkness. The walls were carved with murals — battles between shadow and flame, figures kneeling before a crowned silhouette cloaked in void.

At the center stood a black stone altar surrounded by chains of silver, each link engraved with runes that glowed faintly as they approached.

Veyr's voice was barely a whisper. "I think this is where they bound something."

Lunaris stepped closer. "Or someone."

He brushed the altar's surface — and a rush of energy surged through the room. The murals flickered, and for a moment, all of them saw a figure standing atop a mountain of shadow.

A man in armor darker than night, his face obscured, his eyes burning white.

Malrec.

"The first wielder," Corvus breathed. "The one who tried to tear the Veil open."

The vision faded, leaving only silence. The chains rattled faintly, though no wind stirred.

Lunaris exhaled slowly. "We find the source. Then we end this."

The Whispering Pool

Following the sound of dripping water, they came upon a pool of black liquid that reflected no light. As they approached, their reflections began to change — showing not who they were, but who they could become.

Lunaris saw himself standing atop Everveil's tower, the moon eclipsed behind him, his sword raised as the Veil bowed before his will.
Nyx saw a city in flames, her arrows falling like meteors.
Veyr saw himself surrounded by shadows that bowed when he spoke.
Corvus saw a world without death — silent, still, perfect.

Then, just as quickly, the visions shattered. The pool went still.

"It's testing us," Nyx said.
"Or tempting us," Corvus replied quietly.

They turned to leave — but the path behind them was gone.
The shadows had moved.

The Voice in the Dark

The chamber darkened, and a figure emerged from the far end
of the pool.
Tall, cloaked in a veil of black smoke, its form shifting
between substance and dream.

"Children of Everveil," the voice said, calm and terrible. "You
walk paths you do not yet understand."

Lunaris raised his blade. "Malrec."

The figure tilted its head. "A name the frightened gave their
reflection."

It stepped closer, and for an instant, they saw its face — not
monstrous, but human. A man once like them, eyes hollow
with loss and knowledge.

"You carry what was mine," it said softly. "The relics, the
bloodline, the promise."
"We carry the will to protect the Veil," Lunaris said. "Not
destroy it."
"And yet," Malrec whispered, "every protector becomes the
destroyer in time."

Then the shadows erupted, and the figure vanished, leaving
behind only its echo.

The Ascent

When the Vow finally reached the surface again, the sky
above Duskwood had turned violet. The tear still glowed
faintly, but smaller now — like a wound that had begun to
heal.

They stood in silence at the mouth of the cavern, the wind cold
and heavy with ash.

"He knows us," Corvus said at last.
"No," Lunaris replied quietly. "He's been waiting for us."

They looked back at the darkness they had left behind — and
for the first time, it felt like the darkness was looking back.

Chapter XLII — Whispers of the Broken Veil

The ride back to Everveil was long and silent.
Snow fell in slow spirals, catching the faint glow of the moons
that watched over them like pale sentinels.

Lunaris rode ahead, his cloak heavy with soot and shadow.
Corvus walked beside him, staff resting across his shoulders,
eyes distant. Behind them, Nyx and Veyr carried the recovered
relic shards and essence vials taken from the fallen creatures.

No one spoke.
The silence wasn't discomfort — it was weight. The kind that
came from knowing the world had just shifted beneath them.

When Everveil's towers came into view through the treeline,
their spires were lit with white flame — a signal of ward
activation. The Veil itself shimmered faintly above the school,
as if rippling with unease.

The Headmaster's Summons

They were led directly to the Great Hall upon arrival.
Headmistress **Veyra Norn**, flanked by the seven House heads,
stood at the dais beneath the Everveil crest. The tension in the
room was thick enough to drown in.

"Four students, gone for a week without clearance," said
Master Arlen of the House of Storms. "Then you return with
relics that haven't been touched in centuries."

Corvus bowed his head slightly. "With respect, we didn't go
looking for relics. They found us."

The murmurs began again — incredulous, fearful, hungry. Veyra raised her hand. The chamber fell silent.

Her eyes found Lunaris.

"Tell us what you saw."

Lunaris met her gaze evenly. "A tear in the Veil. Old magic, bound in silver. Something — someone — was imprisoned there. He spoke to us."

The word hung in the air like a curse.

"Malrec."

The name drew a shudder from the room.

"Impossible," whispered Mistress Elowen of the House of Mind. "He was sealed in the Old War."

"Then something's breaking that seal," Lunaris said quietly. "And it's starting from the inside."

The Relic Revelation

Headmistress Veyra stepped down from the dais, her long robes trailing shadow. She moved to the center of the chamber, where the relics had been laid out — weapons forged of blacklight and metal that defied the natural order.

She circled them once, hand hovering over the sword, the staff, the bow, and the twin daggers.

"These aren't relics," she murmured. "They're keys."

The House Masters shifted uneasily.

"Keys to what?" Arlen asked.

"To the gates Malrec sought to open," Veyra said. "And to the power that stopped him."

Her eyes lifted to the Vow.

"The Veil doesn't choose lightly. If these have answered to you, then you are now bound by its will. You are the new Wardens of Shadow."

The torches dimmed as the words settled in. For a moment, the silence was absolute.

The Night Watch

Later, beneath the frost-hung towers, Lunaris stood alone on the balcony of the House of Shadows. The snow reflected the moonlight like scattered glass.

Corvus joined him quietly, the faint smoke of necrotic magic still curling from his fingertips.

"They're scared of us now," he said.
"They should be," Lunaris replied.

Below, the Veil shimmered faintly — not with calm, but with pressure, as if something beneath it was pushing upward.

"You think he's coming through?" Corvus asked.

Lunaris's hand tightened on the hilt of his blade. "No. I think he's already here."

The Dream of Shadows

That night, Lunaris dreamed.
He stood again in the cavern — but the altar was gone.
Instead, there was a throne of black crystal, and seated upon it
was a shadow that wore his own face.

It smiled.

"You think you've chosen the light," the dream said, "but the
darkness remembers its own."

When Lunaris woke, the mark on his shoulder — the one
shaped like a wolf's eye — was burning.

And in the distance, the bells of Everveil began to toll.

Chapter XLIII — The Shadows Stir

The bells of Everveil rang at dawn.
Their sound carried over the mountains like distant thunder —
solemn, hollow, and old. Few students knew what they meant.
Fewer still wanted to.

By midmorning, rumors ran through every corridor: a
forbidden chamber opened, relics awakened, and something in
the Veil had whispered a name.

Malrec.

The Headmasters said nothing.
The council chambers remained sealed.
But the air itself seemed to hum with unease.

The Weight of Secrets

Lunaris moved through the empty courtyard, frost crackling
beneath his boots. His breath misted the air in rhythmic
clouds.
Everywhere, eyes followed him — students whispering behind
walls of ivy and stone.

"That's them — the four from the caverns."
"They say the shadows answered to them."
"They say one of them saw the end of the world."

He didn't respond.
He'd learned quickly that silence was stronger than denial.

At the edge of the courtyard, he found Corvus waiting —
hands clasped behind his back, eyes dark and thoughtful.

“The others are in the lower hall,” Corvus said. “Veyra wants us back by nightfall.”

Lunaris nodded, his gaze shifting toward the northern sky. The light there was strange — thin, flickering, as if fighting to exist. “It’s spreading,” he murmured. “The rifts.”

“And so are the whispers,” Corvus replied. “I heard the House of Mind sealed its archives. They think the prophecy’s been misinterpreted.”

“Prophecies usually are,” Lunaris said quietly. “Until they’re fulfilled.”

The Hidden Lesson

In the lower training hall, Nyx stood before a mirror of obsidian, drawing her bow in slow, deliberate motion. Her reflection shimmered oddly — a second shadow behind her, moving slightly out of sync.

“It’s been doing that since the caverns,” she said without turning.

Veyr, sitting cross-legged nearby, was etching new runes into his gauntlets with a silver stylus. “Your familiar’s reaching for you,” he said. “They always do, once bound through the Veil.”

“You make it sound like a curse.”

“It’s both,” Veyr replied.

Lunaris and Corvus entered as her next arrow struck the bullseye — dead center. The sound echoed like a soft, final heartbeat.

Veyr rose. "What did the council say?"

Lunaris's jaw tightened. "That we're to stay close. Train. Wait."

"Wait for what?" Nyx asked.

He hesitated, then looked toward the window. "For the next breach."

The Rift Report

That night, as the others slept, Lunaris sat alone in the library's highest spire. The room was cold and silent, the air thick with dust and candle smoke.

He opened the latest Veilguard reports — sealed under a sigil he'd broken quietly.
Inside: sketches of spectral entities, sightings in nearby towns, and a final note written in haste.

"The rifts multiply. Shadows bleed through places that should be safe. We fear the name spoken in the dark — Malrec — is not memory, but movement."

Lunaris closed the parchment, his expression unreadable.
Then he heard the soft scrape of boots behind him.

Headmistress Veyra stood in the doorway, her presence quiet but heavy.

"You've seen the reports," she said.
"I had to."
"And what do you believe?"

Lunaris met her eyes. "That the prophecy is already in motion."

Veyra's hand brushed the edge of a nearby tome — *The Chronicles of the Seven Houses.* Her voice was almost a whisper.

"Then perhaps the world will need the Vow sooner than we hoped."

The Flickering Moon

That night, the moon above Everveil dimmed — not by cloud or storm, but by something deeper, as if the Veil itself were breathing.

Down in the courtyard, the torches flickered blue. The students who saw it would later swear they heard whispers — faint, unearthly, like laughter behind glass.

And far to the north, beyond the Cascades, a figure stood in the ruins of a forgotten fortress, watching the light die.

Malrec smiled.

"The Heir has taken his place," he murmured. "Then so shall I."

The wind howled through the mountains, carrying with it a sound that was not quite thunder — and not quite human.

Chapter XLIV — Whispers Beneath the Veil

The morning after the moon dimmed, Everveil felt wrong.
The air carried a cold stillness — as if the mountain itself held its breath. The students went about their classes, but every whisper echoed longer than it should have. The torches along the halls burned low, their flames curling inward instead of out.

From the upper cloister, Lunaris watched the fog roll in from Lake Crescent.
He could feel it — the quiet pull in his chest. The same hum that had called him before the first relic chose him.
Something was stirring again.

The Mission Board

By midday, the summons bell rang through the House of Shadows.
The students gathered in the grand hall, its walls adorned with banners depicting the seven House sigils. The mission board — a towering slab of living obsidian — shimmered with new inscriptions, written in faintly glowing runes.

Headmistress Veyra stood beside it, her eyes hard but calm.

"The Veil has torn again," she announced. "This time near the northern border. Veilguard scouts confirm the corruption spreads through the roots of the forest. Only advanced pairs will be sent. Choose wisely."

The shadows across the board shifted, swirling until one mission burned brighter than the rest — the glyphs reshaping into a sigil Lunaris knew all too well.

The *Umbra* crescent.

Corvus caught his glance. "The shadows have chosen again," he said.

"Then we answer," Lunaris replied quietly.

Behind them, Nyx and Veyr stepped forward. The four stood before the board, the light of the inscription painting their faces in blue and silver.

"Exploration and containment," Nyx read aloud. "An anomaly beneath the Frostmire Caverns."

Veyr's grin was dark and steady. "A cave, again? Guess fate has a sense of humor."

Lunaris's eyes narrowed slightly. "No. This one feels… alive."

Echoes in Stone

Hours later, as twilight fell, the four descended into the Frostmire range — snow drifting like ash around them. Their breath came in visible puffs, illuminated by the sigils etched into their armor.

The entrance lay half-buried beneath the ice — a chasm breathing faint tendrils of violet mist.

Corvus ran a gloved hand along the frozen stone. "This is no natural tear. Something forced it open."

"The same thing that's been watching," Nyx murmured. Her eyes glowed faintly with reflection magic, seeing further into the dark than the others could. "There's movement. Far in."

Lunaris drew his blade. Shadows curled along the edge, whispering softly in an ancient tongue.

"Then let's finish what we started."

The descent began.

The Second Rift

They hadn't been underground ten minutes before the temperature dropped. The air turned heavy, metallic, tasting faintly of blood and magic.

The tunnel opened into a vast cavern, its walls webbed with veins of pulsing light.

Then came the sound — low and guttural, like stone grinding against bone.

A shape moved in the darkness. Massive. Breathing. Watching.

When it stepped into the light, even the Veil itself seemed to recoil.

A **Drakoryn**, half spectral, half flesh — a forgotten beast said to have once served the ancient Shadowlords before the Veil divided the worlds.

Veyr's voice cracked through the silence. "Well. That's new."

The Drakoryn roared — and the cavern trembled.

The Battle of Frostmire

What followed was chaos.
The four scattered as the beast lunged, claws gouging through
black ice. The walls shattered with every strike, sending
shards like razors through the air.

Nyx loosed arrows of molten shadow, each one igniting on
impact.
Corvus summoned spectral chains, binding the creature's legs
long enough for Veyr to strike.
Lunaris leapt forward, blade blazing with violet fire.

The Drakoryn turned — its eyes two pools of void. It spat a
torrent of freezing mist that crystallized the floor in seconds.

"It's drawing from the Veil!" Nyx shouted.
"Then we cut the connection!" Lunaris roared.

He drove his sword deep into the creature's chest, light flaring
along the veins of the cavern.
For a moment, everything froze — silent, blinding, eternal.

Then the Drakoryn screamed. Its body fractured into glasslike
shards, each one glowing faintly before dissolving into mist.

When the light faded, Lunaris was kneeling, his left arm
burning with a new mark — a twisting sigil shaped like the
creature's eye.

The wolf tattoo shimmered, growling faintly before dimming.

"It gave you something," Corvus said quietly.

"No," Lunaris whispered. "It took something."

The Shadow's Gift

When they emerged, dawn had broken. The snow had stopped. Above the mountains, the Veil shimmered faintly — torn, but healing.

Veyr clapped Lunaris on the shoulder. "If every mission's like that, we're gonna need bigger weapons."

"And stronger armor," Nyx added, checking the crack along her bowstring.

Lunaris didn't reply. His hand still glowed faintly, and deep within the mark, the Drakoryn's roar echoed — distant but alive.

He could feel it — something ancient awakening within him, responding to the Veil's call.

And far away, in the shadow between worlds, **Malrec** felt it too.

He smiled in the dark.

"The heir of shadow grows stronger… good. Let him. The fall will be sweeter when it comes."

CHRONICLES OF THE EBON VOW

YEAR I

Everveil Institute Academic Year (Canon Locked)

Current Year: *The Year of the Fractured Veil (Year I of the Ebon V*

SCHOOL YEAR OVERVIEW

Summer (Pre-term)

> July 12: Stephen's 15 Birthday — Shelows first sirr at *Unana estat.* Preparations and summons to EVERVEIL INSTITUTE.

Autumn Term

> Dec, 31: Arrival at Everveil, The frvill: The first cere monts: House assignments, and discovery of the school's hidden depths.

> Nov: 31: Thanksgiving beserves: Thanksgiving observence eves the Crakoryn—the first whispers of Malrec begencs.

Winter Term

> Dec, 1. 1Winter Break:. Stephen return home, receives the Vevail.

> Mid-January: Return to Evervell, first whispers of Malree growe stronger: Late January — Frostmire Covern. Mission —confrontation.

> Early Feburary: Recovery period, new powers and prophecies unfol.

> May 30: End of Term: Annual Closing Ceremony. The Carl's next disturbance—the /Book I clifihanger finale.

CURRENT IN-STORY DATE:

February 6th, Year *of the* Fractured Veil

(Midway through Winter Term—after the Frostmire mission and before the Vell's next disturbance.)

Chapter XLV — Embers Beneath the Ice

The northern winds howled across the tundra like a thousand dying voices. Frozen peaks rose from the mist, jagged and ancient, their spires laced with veins of faint blue light. Snow drifted endlessly, whispering against steel and cloth, the only sound that dared to exist between heartbeats.

The Ebon Vow moved in silence through the ruins of Val'Korran — a sunken temple half-buried in frost and shadow. The Veil had torn wide above it, bleeding black aurora into the northern sky. It pulsed with a rhythm almost alive, casting ghostfire hues across the ice.

"This is worse than what the reports said," murmured **Kael**, his staff leaving trails of pale flame in the snow.
"The reports didn't come from anyone who lived long enough to describe it," **Lunaris** answered, eyes narrowing as the mark on his forearm faintly glowed through his glove — a silver wolf wrapped in shadowfire.

They had seen Veil breaches before. This one *breathed*.

The earth itself seemed to pulse as they descended into the fractured ruin. Jagged spires of frozen stone jutted upward, each humming with faint runes that bled mist. And from that mist came movement — first slow, then all at once.

The first creature burst from beneath the ice — a hulking form of sinew and bone, its chest hollow, its head crowned by horns of frozen light. Others followed: wraith-beasts, revenant shades, creatures half-formed and broken by the Veil's corruption.

"Positions!" Lunaris barked.

The Vow scattered like shadows. **Nyx** raised her arms, song already forming — a low, resonant hum that cracked the frozen air. The sound rolled across the battlefield like a stormfront, shattering the ice beneath their enemies and staggering the front line.

Veyr's serpent familiar coiled around his arm, splitting into twin phantoms of smoke and frost. They struck with blinding speed, tearing into the nearest shade and turning its black ichor into steam.

Kael drove his staff into the snow, releasing a surge of necrotic energy that tore through the wraiths, scattering their forms into drifting ash. His eyes glowed cold white, his voice low: "Return to what the Veil forgot."

The ground cracked beneath them.

From below, a massive claw of ice and bone erupted, seizing the edge of the ruin and pulling up something colossal. A frost-titan — half beast, half spirit — rose into the night, its chest glowing with a hollow blue fire.

It roared, and the auroras flickered like dying stars.

Lunaris' shadowblade burst to life, igniting with mirrored light — half silver, half black. "Vow! On me!"

They struck as one.
Kael hurled necrotic flame, searing the titan's arm; Nyx's sonic wave shattered its armor of ice; Veyr sent his twin serpents to blind it, while Lunaris climbed its back, blade carving glowing sigils with every strike.

When the titan fell, it did not die quietly. The explosion of frost and shadow knocked them flat — and for a moment, everything went still except the whisper of the Veil above.

As they stood amid the ruins, the **shadows moved again**, unbidden. The black mist that had lingered after the fight began to divide and swirl, forming **four equal piles** of gold, crystal, and vein-stone at their feet — spoils of battle, neatly apportioned.

Kael exhaled. "It never stops being eerie when it does that." "Not eerie," Lunaris said, sheathing his blade. "It's recognition. The shadows know who stands in balance."

From within the snow, Nyx uncovered a fragment of obsidian carved with the **Umbra crescent**. She turned it in her gloved hand. "This wasn't made by accident."

Lunaris took it carefully, feeling a pulse deep within the stone — the same resonance that had stirred in the relic chamber months ago. "No," he murmured. "It's a warning. Something's pulling harder from the other side."

They made camp within the broken temple, the Veil breach above dimming to a bruise-colored scar across the sky. The fire burned blue, their shadows long against the ancient walls.

For the first time since the forming of the Vow, none of them spoke.

Outside, the auroras shifted, and for a fleeting instant, the frost on the stones spelled out words in an ancient tongue — the same language that once marked the altar of the relic room.

Kael stared. "Do you see that?"
Lunaris nodded grimly.
It read:

"The ice remembers what the fire forgot."

Chapter XLVI — Whispers Through Frost and Flame

The fire burned low, its embers a faint heartbeat beneath the howling wind.
Around it, the four sat in a silence weighted not by exhaustion, but by revelation. Shadows curled near the edges of the ruin — patient, watching, almost *listening*.

Lunaris turned the obsidian shard over in his hand again. In the dancing light, the Umbra crescent pulsed faintly, like a dying star. The sigil was precise — too deliberate to be coincidence.

Kael's voice broke the quiet.
"You think it's connected to the relic chamber?"

Lunaris nodded, gaze fixed on the stone. "The craftsmanship's the same. The markings follow Umbra symbology — crescent and binding loop. But there's something else. A corruption threading through it."

Nyx leaned forward, the blue flame reflecting in her eyes.
"Then we've seen the first echo of Malrec's influence."

The name hung in the air like frostbite.

Veyr, usually the calmest of them, ran a hand through his hair. "Malrec was supposed to be myth. A Shadowborn that tried to tear through the Veil in the Second Age."
"He wasn't a myth," Lunaris said softly. "He was *sealed*. And seals… weaken."

Outside the ruined archway, the auroras rippled like ink spilled over glass. The Veil wound was closing, but not healing — a scar that pulsed faintly, as if it remembered pain.

Kael stood, his staff flickering dimly. "If Malrec's power is surfacing again, this isn't the last breach we'll see. And the Institute—"
"Won't believe us," Nyx interrupted. "Not until it's on their doorstep."

The fire hissed as the shadows around them shifted. From the dark, shapes rose — not beasts, but tendrils of mist forming into faint, humanoid silhouettes. They bowed once, and in silence, dropped several objects into the snow: shards of crystal, fragments of armor, and slivers of silver etched with ancient text.

The shadows melted away.

"The Veil's recognizing us again," Kael murmured.
"Not recognizing," said Lunaris, his tone distant. "It's warning us."

He gathered the fragments. Each bore the same inscription, broken across the metal:
"…When the moon bleeds silver, and the wolf stands alone, the shadows shall break their chains…"

The words felt like a chill crawling down each of their spines.

"Prophecy?" Veyr asked.
"More like a continuation," Lunaris replied. "The first part was carved on the altar. This... is the rest."

Nyx exhaled slowly. "So we're not done yet."
"We were never meant to be," Lunaris said, eyes narrowing toward the frozen horizon. "The Veil's wounds are testing us — shaping us. This is just the beginning."

The wind shifted, carrying with it a low, resonant hum from far beyond the ruins — a sound that didn't belong to wind, nor beast, but *something older*.

"Let's move," Lunaris said, rising. "We'll return at dawn. The shadows have more to say, and I'd rather not be here when they decide to start speaking louder."

They doused the blue flame, leaving only the pale light of the aurora to guide them back through the snow.

Behind them, as the last ember died, the frost on the stones shimmered once more — revealing a symbol faintly burned into the ice where the fire had been.

A circle.
A crescent moon within.
And beneath it, one word:

"Malrec."

Stephen
Umbra
Nyx
Nyx
Nyx
Corvus

Chapter XLVII — The Shadows Remember

The snow that blanketed the northern ridges of Val'Korran had begun to melt, revealing the bones of the old world beneath. The battle at the ruin had left the Ebon Vow changed — not just in strength, but in something deeper, quieter. The fire they'd built that night had long gone cold, yet its echo still lingered in the marrow of their shadows.

By morning, the light had turned pale gold, sifting through torn clouds like the world itself was waking after a long dream. Lunaris stood alone near the mouth of the ruined temple, his blade — *Umbra's Oath* — resting point-down in the snow. The obsidian metal still hummed with faint light, veins of silver running like frozen lightning through its core.

Kael approached silently, the snow crunching softly under his boots. "You haven't slept," he said.

Lunaris didn't look at him. "Neither have you."

Kael smirked faintly, pulling his cloak tighter. "Someone had to keep watch. In case the frost wraiths decided they weren't finished."

"They weren't after us," Lunaris replied. "They were guarding something."

Kael frowned. "The shard?"

"The shard," Lunaris confirmed, turning it over in his hand. Its runes pulsed weakly, as if breathing. "It's reacting again. Whatever power it carries—it's not done with us yet."

Nyx stepped from the shadows of the nearby archway, her breath fogging in the cold. "You think it's tied to the relics?" she asked, brushing frost from her gauntlet.

"I think it's older," Lunaris said. "Older than Everveil. Older than the Houses."

Veyr joined them, his usual calm replaced by unease. "Then we should take it to the Headmistress. If this thing has ties to the Veil—"

"No," Lunaris interrupted sharply. "Not yet. You saw what happened in the ruin — the way it chose to reveal itself. The shadows moved for *us*, not the council. This is our burden now."

The group fell silent. Even the wind seemed to still, the forest beyond the ridge holding its breath.

Finally, Kael exhaled, rubbing the back of his neck. "You make it sound like destiny."

Lunaris looked toward the mountains, where the first hints of sunlight caught the frost-tipped trees. "Maybe it is. But destiny isn't what binds us — it's the vow we made."

He reached down, pressing a hand into the snow. The frost hissed under his touch as a faint sigil of the Ebon Vow shimmered — seven interlocking marks forming a single ring.

Nyx knelt beside him, tracing one of the glowing lines. "Then we need to find out what the other fragments are," she said. "Before someone else does."

Veyr nodded grimly. "If the shard's energy spreads, the Veil will feel it. And so will whatever's on the other side."

Lunaris stood, gripping his blade. The obsidian light flared — a reflection of the fire in his eyes.

"Then we move," he said. "We hunt the echoes. Every relic, every mark, every shadow that remembers."

As the group turned south toward the mountain pass, a faint whisper drifted through the thawing air — not quite a voice, but the echo of one.

The Vow has awoken. The Balance trembles.

And far beyond the snow and silence, deep within the Veil, something ancient stirre

Chapter XLVIII — The Forging of the Vow

The forge on Market Street burned with silver fire that did not flicker or fade.
It pulsed like a living heart — ancient, patient, and aware.

The Forger, a man as old as shadow, stood before the Ebon Vow without a word. His eyes burned with emberlight, his skin veined with faint silver scars that pulsed in rhythm with the hammer's fall.
He did not ask who they were. The shadows already knew.

Lunaris set down the veilsteel ore and beast hide they'd gathered. Corvus followed, laying the preserved heart of a slain wraith upon the anvil. Nyx brought forth the crystallized ash of a fallen flame-beast, and Veyr placed the shards of obsidian armor cracked during their battle in the caves.

The Forger's gaze passed over each of them before he spoke — a voice rough as broken stone.
"Four walk in shadow where seven are destined to stand."
He lifted the hammer. "Let the forge remember you."

Sparks leapt like stars. Each strike was a heartbeat of the Veil itself — black flame, silver smoke, and sound that felt older than the mountain. The relics came to life beneath his hand:

- **Lunaris's blade**, once a dagger, now a long, crescent-edged sword etched with the words *Veritas in Tenebris*. Its glow shimmered between moonlight and living mist.
- **Corvus's staff**, rebuilt with a spine of bone and veins of glass, whispered faintly in lost tongues.
- **Nyx's bow**, forged from volcanic glass and shadowed ember, burned without consuming itself, its string humming with a low, haunting note.

- **Veyr's twin daggers**, reborn from shattered metal and living shadow, flickered between reality and reflection each time he moved.

The Forger stepped back, sweat running like mercury down his brow.
"These are not weapons," he said. "They are echoes. They know you now. And they will remember."

As the four reached for their relics, light and shadow coiled around them, weaving together into living sigils that marked their wrists. The air trembled.
Lunaris felt the hum deep in his bones — something binding, something eternal.

Corvus's gaze met his. "This isn't just power," he said softly.
Nyx's voice was quieter still. "It's recognition."

Veyr's grin flickered through the dim. "Feels like the Veil just branded us."

Lunaris lifted *Umbra's Oath*, its edge shimmering pale and cold. "Then may the world remember who we are."

The forge burned brighter — shadows rising like wings around them.
The Forger's voice followed, distant and almost reverent:
"The Ebon Vow is reforged."

Chapter XLIX — Shadows and Sparks

The night air above Lake Crescent was razor-thin, clear enough to see the fractured moon reflected in the frozen water below. The four of them stood on the cliff's edge, their breath silver, their relics newly awakened.

No one spoke for a long time.

The relics still hummed with life, their glow painting the snow in shifting hues:

- *Umbra's Oath* bled soft lunar light.
- *Corvus's staff* pulsed in waves, runes circling faintly.
- *Nyx's bow* burned ember-red at the tips, smoke curling from her fingers.
- *Veyr's daggers* shimmered and vanished, reappearing only as faint silhouettes in the mist.

When Lunaris finally moved, his voice was low. "Every time we do this," he said, "it feels like we're being watched."

"Not watched," Corvus murmured. "Acknowledged."

Nyx ran her fingers over the curve of her bow, watching it flicker in and out of sight. "It's the same energy as the chamber. The Veil knows we carry part of it now."

"Good," Veyr said, half a smile on his face. "Then it'll know who to blame when we start rewriting its rules."

Lunaris drove his blade into the snow, the crescent edge catching moonlight. "We've all earned what we hold — and what comes with it. These relics, these familiars, these marks... they bind us tighter than blood."

He looked at each of them in turn.
"Whatever comes next, we face it together — as the Vow."

One by one, the others planted their relics beside his.
The snow beneath their feet shimmered — sigils forming of
their own accord, glowing with power. At the center, the
crescent wolf of the Umbra line took shape, framed by smaller
runes representing raven, serpent, and bat.

The Veil itself seemed to whisper through the ice, a faint echo
rising between the trees.

Corvus stepped forward, placing a gloved hand on Lunaris's
shoulder.
"The world may not know our names," he said, "but it will
know our mark."

Lunaris nodded once. "Truth in shadow. Strength in
darkness."

The relics pulsed in unison.
Snow spiraled upward in a slow, soundless storm.
And the four of them stood at its center — silent, eternal,
unbroken.

The Ebon Vow had been reforged,
and the world had begun to take notice.

Chapter L — The Oath Beneath the Moon

Morning came slow, silver, and cold.
Mist clung to the treetops below the cliffs, winding through
the pines like breath from the sleeping world. The Ebon Vow
had not slept. None of them dared to.

The forge marks were still warm on their skin.
Lunaris sat by the fire's dying embers, *Umbra's Oath* resting
across his knees, the metal faintly glowing even in the light of
dawn. The others were scattered around the clearing — silent,
watchful, lost in their thoughts.

Nyx was first to speak. "It's louder today," she whispered.

Veyr looked up from the twin daggers he was cleaning. "What
is?"

"The Veil," she said. "It's like it's breathing."

Corvus's spectral raven — *Noctra* — stirred upon his
shoulder, feathers glimmering faintly. "It's reacting to the
binding," Corvus murmured. "Four relics awakened, one oath
reforged. It's not used to being… remembered."

Lunaris raised his gaze to the horizon. The clouds over the
valley pulsed faintly — not with sunlight, but shadowlight, the
faint echo of the realm between. "Then we've stirred it," he
said. "And that means someone else can feel it too."

"The Headmasters?" Veyr asked.

Lunaris shook his head. "No. Something older."

Silence fell again — the kind that seemed to have weight.

The shadows of the trees began to stretch in unnatural directions, bending toward the four of them like strings being pulled taut. The sigils on their arms glowed in unison. The same whisper reached them all at once — not in words, but in meaning:

Oath and blood. Flame and frost. Four awaken where seven are bound.

Corvus's eyes flickered open. "It's marking us again."

Nyx shivered. "It feels like being watched by the moon itself."

Lunaris rose, gripping the sword's hilt. "Then we give it something worth watching."

He stepped into the clearing's center, moonlight spilling through the thinning mist. "Last night, we forged our weapons," he said. "But that wasn't the end of the vow — it was the beginning."

He turned slowly to face them, the others rising one by one. "We've all taken oaths before — to the Houses, to our bloodlines, to the school. But this one is different. This one belongs to us."

Veyr smirked faintly. "You're not exactly the praying type, Lunaris."

"Neither are you," Lunaris said. "That's why it'll work."

He raised *Umbra's Oath*. The other three followed, crossing relics at the blade's center — the bowstring, the staff's tip, the twin daggers' edges, all meeting in silence.

The moon above dimmed — or perhaps the world simply grew darker to make room for what they were about to become.

Lunaris's voice was low but steady. "By shadow and by truth, we swear — to never wield these weapons in greed, nor in vengeance, but in defense of those who cannot stand alone."

The Veil stirred.
Corvus's staff flared white. "To protect the balance between realms," he added, his tone like a promise carved in bone.

Nyx's eyes burned ember-red. "To never let the fire of power blind us to the light that still remains."

Veyr finished, quiet but sharp. "And to never forget that shadows walk beside every heart — even our own."

The four relics pulsed once, twice — then fused in light so bright the snow turned to steam. A ring of sigils burned into the ground, linking them together in one shared mark.

When it faded, the clearing was still.
The air was clear again. The world — momentarily — at peace.

Lunaris looked down at the sigil beneath their feet.
It was a perfect crescent, surrounded by seven empty runes.
"Four of seven," he murmured. "The prophecy's counting."

Nyx's voice trembled slightly. "Then three more are still out there."

"Then we find them," Lunaris said. "Before something else does."

The others nodded, silent understanding passing between them.

Above them, the fractured moon shone through the thinning clouds, and for the first time since the forging, the shadows bent not in threat — but in allegiance.

The Ebon Vow was complete in its beginning.
And far beyond Everveil, in a place the sun could not reach, something stirred — smiling.

Chapter LI — Shadows Unbound

The night air at Frostline burned with cold, but the shadows pulsed with heat.
Lunaris stood amid the ruins of the battle, the moon a fractured disc above the mountains. His cloak was torn, his blade slick with ichor that shimmered like smoke.

Around him, the others caught their breath — **Corvus** leaning on his staff, **Veyr** sheathing his daggers with hands still trembling, and **Nyx** drawing her bowstring taut one last time before letting the tension ease.

They had won, but not cleanly.

The frost had melted where Lunaris's sword struck, the ground beneath him seared in the shape of a crescent. His shadow familiar — the great silver-eyed wolf — lingered nearby, pacing between pools of melted snow and blackened stone. Its breath fogged the air in tendrils that glowed faintly blue.

"He's adapting," Corvus muttered. "The wolf. It didn't do that before."

Lunaris's gaze didn't shift. "Neither did I."

The weight of his power sat uneasily in his chest — an echo of something ancient and half-remembered. When he closed his eyes, he saw the shape of Malrec's mark burning through the ice: a spiral of teeth and flame.

They gathered the relic shards and returned to camp. The fire burned low, its smoke curling into strange shapes. For a long time, none of them spoke.

Then Nyx broke the silence. "He's testing us."

"Malrec?" Veyr asked.

"No." Her eyes found Lunaris across the firelight. "The Veil."

Lunaris didn't argue. Somewhere deep inside, the wolf growled — not in anger, but in agreement.

"Then we test it back," he said.

And in the flicker of that moment, all four shadows lengthened — moving with a life that was no longer just their own.

Chapter LII — The Weight of Flame

They returned to Everveil under a sky that bled fire.
The horizon shimmered with strange auroras — ripples of Veil
energy visible even to the powerless. Bells rang in the distant
towers, but no one celebrated.

Within the walls of the House of Shadows, the air was thick
with whispers. The corridors were quieter than usual, the
torches burning blue instead of gold. The old stones
remembered what had happened at Frostline — the tremor that
had rippled through the Veil itself.

Lunaris stood before the grand hearth of the common hall,
hands clasped behind his back. The Umbra Crest — the wolf
and crescent — gleamed faintly above the mantle.
It had never looked so heavy.

"We didn't fail," Corvus said quietly beside him. "But we
didn't win either."

Lunaris's eyes reflected the fire. "The Veil doesn't care about
victories. It cares about balance."

Nyx sat at one of the long tables, sketching new arrow sigils
on parchment. "Balance isn't holding. You've felt it — the
pulse in the walls, the flicker in the wards. Something's
breaking."

Veyr leaned against the doorway, his voice low. "Then maybe
it's time we stop pretending this is just a school."

That drew their gazes. For a moment, the four of them simply
stared at one another — aware, in a way they hadn't been
before, that the line between student and sentinel had already
blurred.

Lunaris turned to the fire and drew his blade. The crescent marking along the edge shimmered faintly, whispering in the old tongue of the Umbra Clan. He could feel his father's voice in it — **Cael Umbra's** teaching, the shadow of the oath he'd carried long before his son was born.

"Then we become what we were meant to be," Lunaris said softly.
"Not students. Not soldiers. Shadows unbound."

The others nodded, and as the firelight burned, their reflections darkened — shapes no longer wholly human.

Outside, snow began to fall again, glowing faintly blue where it touched the wards.

Chapter LIII — The Return to Everveil

The mountain mists parted by morning.

By the time the sun crept over the horizon, Everveil's spires shimmered through the veil of fog — silver towers glinting like old memories. The air smelled of rain and iron, the familiar weight of the school pressing against the world as if it had been waiting for them to return.

Lunaris and the others trudged up the cobbled road that wound toward the main gate. Their cloaks were torn, armor dulled by battle and travel, but the shadows still moved with them — loyal, living things drawn to their pulse. The gate guards stiffened at the sight of them; word of the Frostline Pass had already spread through the halls like wildfire.

They were not students returning from a mission.
They were myths coming home.

Inside the courtyard, bells tolled low and heavy, announcing the return of the Ebon Vow. Students paused mid-step, whispering as they passed. Even some of the upper-years bowed their heads, out of respect or fear — it was hard to tell which.

Corvus rolled his shoulders, cracking the stiffness from his neck. "Feels like we've been gone a century."

"Feels like we brought a century back with us," Veyr muttered, gaze flicking toward the shimmering wards above the towers. They flickered faintly — too faintly — as though still recovering from the surge that had shaken the mountains.

Nyx was quiet, her eyes following the ravens that circled the far tower. "The Veil's thinner now. Even here."

Lunaris didn't answer. He could feel it too — a soft pull beneath his skin, like the breath of something vast inhaling. His wolf stirred within the shadow mark on his chest, restless.

Headmistress Veyra was waiting for them in the Grand Hall. The stained glass cast her in gold and violet light, her expression unreadable. She rose as they entered.

"Lunaris. Corvus. Nyx. Veyr." Her voice carried the weight of tradition and exhaustion in equal measure. "You've returned from Frostline."

Lunaris nodded, setting a blackened satchel on the table before her. "And not empty-handed. We found fragments — sigils carved into the ice. Malrec's markings."

At the name, the room darkened — or perhaps it only felt that way.

Veyra's jaw tightened. "The council feared as much. You will rest tonight. Tomorrow, you will debrief. After that... the examinations begin."

"Already?" Corvus frowned. "We barely made it back alive."

"The Veil doesn't wait for comfort," Veyra said, her tone softening only slightly. "Nor will your enemies."

Nyx's lips curved faintly. "We wouldn't want it any other way."

They were dismissed with quiet ceremony, but the hall lingered behind them — whispers, glances, and the flicker of candlelight catching on the sigil of the House of Shadows above the archway.

Outside, the wind howled across the parapets.

Lunaris stood there for a long time after the others had gone, staring down at the training grounds below, now empty and silent. The same grounds where he had first fumbled a spell, where Kael had laughed, where everything had seemed simpler.

The wolf mark pulsed faintly under his shirt — not painful, but aware.

"You feel it too," he murmured. "Something's coming."

A voice drifted from behind him — Nyx's, quiet as moonlight. "It always is."

She joined him at the balcony rail, eyes on the distant mists. The two of them stood together, not speaking. Below them, the torches of Everveil burned through the fog, small but defiant.

For now, the storm had passed.

But in the heart of the mountain, beneath the lowest vaults of Everveil, the ancient wards of the school trembled once — as though something vast and unseen had brushed against them from the other side of the Veil.

And in that brief vibration, a whisper echoed through the dark:

"The hour draws near, Lunaris-born. Shadows remember their heirs."

Chapter LIX — Veilfire Rising

The bells of Everveil tolled thirteen times at dawn.
Their echo rolled across the mountain like thunder, stirring the fog that clung to the spires. It was the call for **Final Examinations**, though everyone knew this year's trials would be unlike any before.

Lunaris stood in the courtyard with the others as the banners of the seven Houses rippled in the pale morning wind. His gaze lifted to the obsidian tower of the Headmistress, where faint traces of blue light shimmered in the uppermost windows — the sign that the Veilwatch was active again.

"Feels like the mountain's holding its breath," Corvus murmured, tightening his gloves.
"It's not the mountain," Nyx replied. "It's the Veil."

The air itself hummed — not quite sound, not quite silence — like the deep resonance before lightning strikes. Even Veyr, who was never easily unnerved, shifted his weight and cast a glance toward the sealed chamber doors beneath the eastern wing.

The **Veilfire** was waking.

That name was whispered only by the older instructors, in the same tone priests used for curses. It was said to be the raw essence of the Veil itself — the living current that pulsed beneath Everveil's foundations, the same force that had once crowned its founders in shadowlight.

And now, for the first time in generations, it stirred.

The Call to the Great Hall

At noon, the student body assembled in the **Grand Hall**,
where the banners of all seven Houses hung motionless. The
atmosphere was electric — not of excitement, but of dread and
awe.

Headmistress **Veyra Corven** stood before them, her staff
aglow with faint violet sigils.

"The Veil is thinning again," she said, her voice carrying with
unnatural resonance. "The storms over the Cascade Range are
no longer natural — they are ripples of the breach we sealed
last winter. The Council of the Veil demands investigation."

A murmur rippled through the crowd.
Even the Veilguard, lined along the outer wall, looked uneasy.

Lunaris exchanged a glance with Nyx, who gave a subtle nod.
He didn't need words to know what she was thinking — *this is
it.*

Veyra's gaze fell upon them. "Four students, marked by relic
and prophecy, will accompany the Guard to the source of the
disturbance. The council does not approve… but the Veil itself
has already chosen."

She lifted her hand. The shadows near Lunaris, Nyx, Corvus,
and Veyr rippled — rising from the floor like sentient smoke.

"The Ebon Vow," she said quietly. "You are called again."

Preparations

That night, the forges on Market Street roared to life once
more.
The Forger worked in silence as the Vow stood by, their new

relics glinting in the orange light. The air smelled of metal and rain.

"You're early for heroes," the old man said, eyes gleaming beneath soot-streaked brows. "Or late for survivors. Either way — the Veil knows your names now. It doesn't forget."

He handed Lunaris a blade newly reforged — the same steel he'd carried since the first mission, now laced with fragments of something darker. The crescent on its hilt gleamed like a sliver of moonlight.

"A final shaping before the storm," said the Forger.
"Then we meet it," Lunaris answered.

By the time they left Market Street, the air was alive with static. Lightning danced above the mountains, flashing violet instead of white. The Veilfire storms had begun.

The Whisper Beneath the Stone

Deep in the night, as the Institute slept, Lunaris awoke to the sound of whispering — not words, but motion.
The silver mark across his chest burned faintly. He rose from his bed, the shadows bending as if to clear his path.

He followed them through the dormitory halls, down the staircases, into the oldest wing of the school — the **Archive of Silence**, where no sound could exist without permission.
There, beneath a mural of the seven Houses entwined, a faint light pulsed from a crack in the stone.

He knelt beside it.

From within, something vast looked back — not with eyes, but with presence.
A thought brushed against his mind like cold breath.

"Lunaris-born. The Veil unravels. The heir must choose: to bind it... or to break it."

The words weren't heard — they were *remembered*, as if they had always been there.

Lunaris's hand hovered over the fissure. The stone was warm. He could sense the others even from here — Nyx dreaming of fire, Corvus whispering in his sleep, Veyr sharpening his blades until dawn.

"Not yet," he murmured to the voice.
"The Vow stands together."

The whisper receded, leaving only the faint pulse of Veilfire beneath the floor.

When Lunaris stood again, the mural seemed to shift.
The crescent of the Umbra glowed faintly, and beside it — faintly visible now — an eighth sigil, one that no one had ever recorded: **a flame wrapped in shadow**.

Chapter LX — The Breath of the Veil

The morning mist clung low over the academy grounds, thin as gauze yet heavy with the taste of static. Lunaris stood beside the black-lacquered railing of the courtyard bridge, his breath fogging in the chill air. Below, the waterfalls of Duskvale thundered down into the gorge — louder than usual, almost agitated.

The bells tolled twice.
Finals week had begun.

The Veil hung still and silent in the skies above, yet every student at Everveil could feel it watching. The Veilfire storms that had once licked the mountain's crown had gone dark, but their echoes remained in the tremor of the halls, in the silver sheen that clung to every pool of water when the moon rose.

"Feels like the calm before something bigger," Corvus said quietly, stepping up beside Lunaris. His cloak caught the wind, raven crest gleaming like ink under dawnlight.
"It always does," Lunaris replied. "The Veil never sleeps. It just waits."

From behind them came the muffled sound of laughter — Nyx and Veyr sparring near the edge of the training circle. Her obsidian bow sang through the air with each draw, while Veyr ducked beneath a sweeping arrow, grinning. His twin daggers glinted with new sigils etched along the blades — remnants of their last mission, the cave that had changed everything.

Nyx loosed another arrow that split the air between them. It embedded itself into a training post, bursting into blue flame before fading to smoke.

"Your aim's improving," Veyr teased, brushing ash off his sleeve.
"Your arrogance isn't," she shot back, smirking.

Their laughter felt like something sacred in a world too heavy with prophecy.

The Headmistress's Summons

By afternoon, a summons came through the crystal conduits lining the hallways — faint voices echoing through the shadows. The Vow was to report to the **Veilwatch Tower**.

When they arrived, Headmistress Veyra stood before the great panoramic window overlooking the valley, her reflection a ripple in the dark glass.

"Your examinations are not suspended," she began, her tone as cool as obsidian. "But you will not take them in the same manner as the others."

She turned. The amethyst gem atop her staff pulsed faintly, resonating with their relics.

"You have been chosen to conduct a field assessment — one that will determine whether your bond to the Veil remains stable after your awakening."

"Meaning?" Corvus asked, though his voice betrayed that he already knew.

"Meaning," she said, "you'll be tested beyond the walls. There is a tear forming in the Duskwood — a small one. The Veilguard cannot be everywhere at once."

Lunaris exchanged a look with Nyx, whose expression was unreadable.

"If we go," he said, "and if the Veil responds—"

"Then the prophecy accelerates," Veyra finished, her voice lowering. "And we will have no choice but to call upon the others."

A beat of silence hung between them.

"Then we'll handle it," Lunaris said simply.

The Headmistress inclined her head. "As I suspected you would."

Duskwood, Revisited

That night, the four of them descended the forest paths under the silver of the crescent moon. The trees whispered in voices that were almost words, and the fog seemed to follow their steps.

"Feels different," Veyr muttered.
"It is different," Nyx replied. "The Veil remembers us."

They reached the clearing where the first Veil breach had once glimmered months ago. Now the air shimmered again — a wound of light hovering inches above the earth, pulsing like a heartbeat.

Lunaris felt the familiar burn along his chest — the mark of the Umbra igniting faintly in answer. He extended his hand, and shadows curled around it like smoke.

"This is where it began," he said. "And where it might begin again."

The wound widened slightly at his words.
From within came a whisper — not a voice this time, but a pulse that all four could feel deep in their bones.

Then the wind shifted.
The glow darkened.
The **Veil breathed out**.

Shadows erupted from the tear — liquid and luminous all at once, forming shapes that flickered between beast and memory. The Vow spread out instinctively, weapons drawn, relics gleaming.

Corvus's twin daggers ignited in cold fire.
Nyx's arrows blazed like glass shards.
Veyr vanished in a ripple of mist and reappeared behind a creature, driving his blades through its chest.
Lunaris drew his sword, the crescent etched into the steel flaring to life.

The creatures shrieked — but not in rage.
In warning.

"They're not attacking," Nyx realized.
"They're fleeing," said Corvus.
"From what?" Veyr hissed.

And then — silence.
The shadows withdrew, the Veillight dimming until only embers floated in the air.

From the darkness beyond the breach came a voice none of them had heard before.
Smooth.

Measured.
Too calm to be human.

"The heirs have awakened," it said. "Good."

The voice dissolved into smoke, leaving only the echo of its presence.

Lunaris sheathed his sword. His pulse thundered.

"Malrec," he said.

The others didn't argue.

Chapter LXI — The Echo of Malrec

The shadows of Everveil were never still.
Even when the halls were empty and the Veilfire lamps
burned low, something breathed between the stones — a
sound just beyond hearing, a movement just beyond sight.

Lunaris could feel it.

He sat alone in the Dormitory of the Obsidian Wing, the
moonlight spilling through the lattice window like melted
silver. The crescent mark across his chest glowed faintly,
pulsing with an uneven rhythm that matched neither heartbeat
nor breath. He had not slept since they'd returned.

On the desk before him lay an old tome, its cover bound in
pale leather and sealed with a sigil in the shape of an eye. The
Chronicles of the Veilguard, a record of all breaches ever
sealed in the Pacific Northwest.
The ink on the newest entry hadn't yet dried.

*Duskwood Anomaly — Unknown Origin. Residual energy
suggests sentient manipulation. No casualties. Four student
witnesses under observation.*

Lunaris's fingers tightened around the page. "Sentient
manipulation." The words echoed like a whisper of what they
had seen — or rather, what had seen them.

The Hall of Mirrors

The next morning, the council summoned them again. The
Hall of Mirrors — a chamber reserved for the most delicate
matters of Veilcraft — shimmered with reflected light.
Headmistress Veyra stood at the center, surrounded by

floating shards of glass that projected ghostly images of their battle in the Duskwood. The shadows of the beasts moved, replaying fragments of the event, flickering like memories.

"We analyzed the residue left at the breach," she said. "What you encountered was not merely a tear in the Veil. It was a probe."

Corvus frowned. "A probe… like something searching?"

"Or someone," Veyra corrected. "Whatever lies beyond the Veil is not content to remain hidden. The name you spoke — *Malrec* — has not been uttered in this realm for centuries."

Lunaris stepped forward. "Who was he?"

The Headmistress's eyes darkened.

"Not who. What. Malrec was a construct — the Veil's first mistake. A shadow given thought. A reflection that learned to hunger."

Silence fell over the room like a weight.

Nyx's hand twitched near her bowstring. "And if it's back?"

"Then your time here has shortened considerably," Veyra replied. "The prophecy of the Ebon Vow is not an allegory anymore. It's a summons."

The Dormitory After Dusk

Later that night, the four gathered in their quarters, too restless to sleep. The relics they had claimed from the cavern rested

against the wall, their faint runes breathing light in rhythm
with one another.

Veyr leaned back in his chair, exhaling. "So, the thing in the
woods wants us dead, or worse."

Corvus crossed his arms. "It said *heirs*. That means it knows
what we are."

Nyx's voice was quiet. "Or who we'll become."

Lunaris didn't speak at first. He stared at the flame of the
candle between them — the way it bent, as though bowing to
an unseen wind.
When he finally spoke, his voice was low.

"Then we train harder. We learn faster. If the Veil's watching,
let it see we're not afraid."

The candle flickered — once, twice — and then steadied.
The shadows on the wall seemed to ripple like they were
listening.

The Whispering Glass

As they dispersed to their rooms, Lunaris passed by the
narrow corridor lined with ancient mirrors — relics of the first
headmasters. He paused when his reflection didn't quite match
his movement.

He stepped closer.
The reflection smiled back a moment too late.

Then it spoke — his own voice, but colder, deeper.

"You think you command the darkness," it murmured. "But it remembers its first master."

The glass cracked. The reflection vanished.
Only Lunaris remained, his heart hammering in the quiet.

He didn't notice that behind him, in the dim hallway light, the mirror mended itself — slowly, perfectly — until no trace of the fracture remained.

Chapter LXII — The Mirror's Breath

Morning broke over Everveil beneath a blanket of rolling fog, pale and cold as ash.
The castle's towers cut through the mist like the ribs of a great beast, their windows glowing faintly with candlelight. The air itself seemed to hum — as though the Veil were breathing just beyond the mortal world.

Lunaris hadn't slept.
Every time he closed his eyes, he saw it again — his reflection, smiling from the other side of the glass. Not a dream, not a memory, but something else. A *presence.* One that whispered his name like it already owned it.

The Gathering in the Archives

By dawn, the four members of the Vow gathered deep beneath the school, in the **Archives of Shade** — a massive, circular chamber ringed with forgotten relics and veiled mirrors. Lanterns burned low, casting amber light over shelves lined with tomes that hummed faintly, as if remembering their own words.

Corvus leaned against a cracked marble column, arms folded, shadows flickering around his boots. "You look like death, Lunaris. You sure this isn't just exhaustion talking?"

Lunaris's gaze was fixed on the mirror in the center of the room — an ancient, twelve-foot glass framed in obsidian. "No," he said quietly. "It was real. Something reached through."

Nyx's voice was soft but sharp. "Through the mirrors?"

He nodded once.

Veyr crouched beside one of the smaller mirrors lining the wall, rubbing his thumb across the dust. "Headmistress Veyra said these mirrors used to resonate with the Veil — long before they were sealed."

"Resonate?" Corvus muttered. "You mean they *listened.*"

Before anyone could answer, the glass began to tremble.

The Voice Behind the Glass

The light dimmed.
The reflections in every mirror shifted — not showing the four students, but the room itself, empty and flickering.
Then, from within the largest mirror, a shape began to form.
Smoke bled from the edges of the glass, crawling outward like veins of shadow.

A voice came through — layered, distant, both male and female at once.

"The seal weakens… the heir awakens. The Vow stirs, and so too does He."

The reflection's outline solidified, taking on the silhouette of a tall figure cloaked in endless dark — the faint shimmer of eyes like burning glass glinting through.

Nyx drew her bow, an arrow of living flame notched and ready.
Corvus stepped forward beside Lunaris, blade drawn, the edge of his dagger reflecting the ghost's shifting form.

Veyr raised one hand, murmuring a nullbind — a silencing weave.

But Lunaris didn't move. His reflection was staring straight at him… and smiling.

"You wear his blood, child of Umbra," the voice said.
"And soon, you will wear his crown."

The mirrors around them **shattered outward** in a thunderclap of energy.
Shards froze midair — suspended, glimmering with moonlight and memory. Every fragment showed a different vision: the Duskwood, the Veil, the wolf of shadow standing beside him beneath two moons.

A single shard struck Lunaris's palm.
He gasped as the pain seared through his hand — not a wound, but a *mark*.

A circle with an eye at its center burned into his flesh.

The Brand of the Mirror

Nyx rushed to him. "Lunaris!"
He opened his hand; there was no blood — only a faintly glowing sigil, silver-blue against his skin.

Veyr stepped closer, brow furrowed. "That's not shadowcraft."

Corvus's voice was low. "That's a mark. Something ancient."

Lunaris looked down at the eye symbol, and for a moment he saw it blink.

"It's watching me," he whispered.

As he spoke, Ashael stirred — the great silver-eyed wolf fading from the shadows behind him. The beast pressed its head against Lunaris's arm, hackles raised, a low growl vibrating the air.

The mark pulsed once, then dimmed.

Lunaris closed his fist. "It's Malrec. He's testing the boundary."

The Choice Beneath the Moon

That night, the Ebon Vow stood together in the courtyard. Snow fell in lazy spirals, glowing faintly under the moon. Each of their familiars lingered nearby — Ashael pacing around Lunaris, Noctra perching on Corvus's shoulder, Ryn crouched silently behind Veyr, and Cael curling around Nyx's feet in a ring of emberlight.

Corvus broke the silence. "If this is what he wants — if he's calling you — we answer it. Together."

Nyx nodded. "The four of us."

Veyr smirked, eyes glowing faintly. "If this is how the year ends, at least it'll make for a hell of a story."

Lunaris looked toward the northern horizon, where a faint shimmer lit the mountains like distant lightning.

"Then we go at dawn," he said. "Before the mirror calls again."

Ashael lifted his head, eyes reflecting the moon.
In their depths, Lunaris saw it — the same crescent, the same wolf's silhouette that had burned on the mirror's surface.

And somewhere beyond the walls of Everveil, **something watched back.**

Chapter LXIII — The Mark of the Veil

The morning came cold and silver, the kind of winter light that made everything feel half-dreamed. The frost clung to Everveil's towers like veins of crystal, and the banners of the seven Houses stirred in a wind that wasn't really there.

Lunaris hadn't spoken since the mark appeared. The faint sigil of an eye still glowed dimly beneath the glove he now wore, pulsing like a heartbeat that wasn't his.

The Council's Summons

By midday, the summons came.
A raven — black-feathered, eyes burning faint white — landed on the sill of the House of Shadows' dining hall and dropped a scroll sealed in silver wax.

Corvus was the one who caught it midair. "Headmistress Veyra," he read aloud. "She wants to see us. All of us."

Nyx's eyes narrowed. "Already? Word travels fast."

"Or," Veyr muttered, finishing his cup, "the Veil told her."

They moved through the halls in silence, the old stones echoing beneath their boots. When they reached the upper chambers, the Headmistress was already waiting by the great arched window that looked out over the valley — a figure of quiet power in deep silver robes.

"Close the door," she said without turning.

They obeyed.

Veyra's reflection glimmered faintly in the window. "You felt it, didn't you, Umbra?"
Lunaris's voice was low. "Yes, ma'am."

"The mark," she said, still facing the glass. "It's not a curse. It's a beacon. The Veil is calling you."

Nyx stepped forward. "Then we silence it."

Veyra finally turned. Her eyes — one gold, one gray — fixed on the four of them. "You can't silence the Veil. But you can learn what it wants."

She opened her hand. Inside was a sliver of obsidian — a mirror shard that pulsed faintly with the same blue light as the mark on Lunaris's palm.

"This came from the Hall of Reflections last night," she said. "Every mirror shattered… except one. The one that bears your name."

Lunaris's chest tightened. "What do you want us to do?"

"Go back," she said simply. "But this time, take control of what looks back."

The Descent

Night fell early that day. The moon hung low, veiled behind streaks of violet cloud. The Vow descended into the lower wings of the school — places even most teachers never entered.

Their path was lit by witchlamps flickering along the walls, burning with faint silver flame.

Corvus ran a hand along one of the old doors. "Feels different tonight."

"It *is* different," Nyx murmured. "The Veil's awake."

They reached the chamber of mirrors again. The shards they'd shattered had reassembled themselves, hovering in perfect symmetry around the largest one — the central glass now swirling with faint mist.

Lunaris drew a breath and stepped forward.

The mark on his hand began to glow.

Through the Reflection

The surface rippled, and before any of them could react, the mirror pulled them through.
For a heartbeat, there was no air, no sound — only weightless shadow and the faint pulse of their own thoughts echoing back.

When the world reformed, they were standing in a place that looked like Everveil — but hollow.
The towers were translucent. The sky was glass. And the ground beneath their feet reflected them twice — once true, once inverted.

"This isn't the Veil," Veyr whispered. "This is its memory."

Something moved through the false horizon — silhouettes walking through walls of glass, each bearing faces the Vow recognized: students, teachers, even themselves. But their reflections *didn't* move with them.

Nyx nocked an arrow of light. "Whatever this place is, it's not ours."

A low growl rose behind them. Ashael emerged, fur dark as ink, eyes burning like silver fire. His hackles lifted as he stared into the reflection of the false Everveil — and there, mirrored perfectly, was another wolf.
Identical.
But its eyes burned *red*.

The Reflection's Trial

The ground split. Mirrors cracked.
Each of them was suddenly facing their reflection — perfect copies that moved just out of sync, wielding shadowed versions of their weapons.

Lunaris's reflection spoke first. "You can't lead what you don't understand."

Corvus's reflection smirked. "You hide from what you already are."

Nyx's twin whispered. "You'll burn the world before you save it."

Veyr's double said nothing — only stared, serpent eyes blank and endless.

Then the reflections *attacked*.

The clash was silent but brutal — soundless strikes echoing in the air like ripples in water. Ashael lunged at his mirror-self, jaws locking with its ghostly counterpart. Lunaris swung his blade, the mark on his hand flaring with every strike.

He felt it then — the pulse of the Veil moving through him, each heartbeat aligning with the shadow. He stopped fighting the reflection and began *mirroring* it — each movement perfect, synchronized. The two Lunaris figures moved in harmony until, finally, they merged into one.

The mark on his hand flared white, and the false Everveil shattered around them.

The Return

When they awoke, they were lying on the floor of the Archives, the mirror before them cracked down the middle. Snow drifted through the shattered window above. The chamber was silent except for the faint hum of the runes carved into the walls.

Corvus sat up first. "We won?"

"No," Lunaris said softly. "We were *measured.*"

Nyx turned toward him. "By what?"

He looked at his palm. The mark was gone — replaced by a faint scar shaped like a crescent over an eye.
"The Veil knows who we are now," he said. "And it's watching."

Ashael padded to his side, brushing against him. For the first time since the mirror incident, Lunaris felt calm.

"Then we watch back," Corvus said, rising. "We're the Vow. That's what we do."

They walked out into the night, snow swirling through the broken arches of Everveil — four shadows beneath a fractured moon.

Chapter LXIV — The Echo Between Worlds

The days that followed passed like fragments of a dream.
Everveil had returned to its usual rhythm — lessons resumed,
the bells of the Great Hall tolled at dusk, and the shadows that
haunted the lower halls seemed, at least for now, to rest.

But something unseen lingered. The mark might have
vanished from Lunaris's palm, yet he could still feel its echo
thrumming beneath his skin — faint, like a whisper at the edge
of thought.

The Veil wasn't silent.
It was *listening*.

The Headmistress's Warning

On the morning of the third day, Lunaris was summoned
alone.
He entered the high tower chamber where Headmistress Veyra
kept her study — a room filled with silvered glass, tomes
bound in obsidian leather, and a vast circular window that
looked toward the northern horizon.

She stood before it, staff in hand, her reflection flickering
faintly in the glass like two images out of alignment.

"You've changed," she said without turning.

"I didn't choose to," Lunaris replied.

"None of us do." She turned then, the silver streaks in her dark
hair catching the light. "The Veil has *chosen you.* That means

it will test you again. It never grants power freely — only bargains.”

Lunaris's jaw tightened. “And what does it want?”

“Balance,” she said softly. “Or perhaps dominion. The difference depends on who's holding the blade.”

Veyra stepped closer, lowering her voice. “You'll start to feel it soon — the pull between what you are and what the Veil wants you to become. When that happens, don't let it speak through you.”

He frowned. “Why tell me this?”

“Because,” she said, “I once heard it speak too.”

Before he could ask, she placed a hand on his shoulder — brief, grounding, almost human — and dismissed him.

He left with more questions than answers.

Reflections and Restlessness

That night, the Vow gathered in the old west courtyard, where the moonlight spilled through the bare branches of the ash trees.
Veyr had dragged a few practice dummies from the training hall, insisting they sharpen their coordination again.

“After that mirror stunt,” he said, tightening his gloves, “we could use some grounding.”

Corvus smirked. “You mean after *you* nearly fell through the glass again.”

Nyx shot a faint ember-tipped arrow into the air, the light flickering across their faces. "Stop bickering. We fight better when we're focused."

Ashael paced behind Lunaris, his massive frame half-shadow, half-silver light. The wolf's eyes glowed brighter tonight — and when Lunaris looked into them, he saw not his reflection, but the faint shimmer of another world behind it.

The connection between them had deepened. He could feel Ashael's instincts pulsing through him — wild, fierce, protective — but beneath it all, something colder. Something watching.

Dreams of the Veil

That night, sleep didn't come easily.
When it did, it brought the Veil.

He dreamed of standing in the mirror realm again, surrounded by endless reflections.
Only this time, there were *no doubles* — just countless images of himself, each marked differently, each holding a weapon that glowed faintly in the dark.

Then, from the center of the mirrored plain, a figure stepped forward — cloaked in living shadow, his eyes identical to Lunaris's own.

"The Vow has been named," the figure said. "But names are promises, and promises demand payment."

"What are you?" Lunaris asked.

"The part of you that remembers what the others forgot."

As the reflection spoke, the ground cracked beneath them, and
the mirrors began to melt into smoke.
From the fog rose seven symbols — the sigils of the Houses
— and at their center, a single crescent of silver flame.

"He is coming," the voice whispered, "and you are his gate."

The mirrors shattered — and Lunaris woke, breath sharp, the
scent of smoke still hanging in the air.

The Whisper in the Hall

When dawn came, the castle was still.
He walked the corridors alone, the cold stone echoing beneath
his boots. The torches flickered strangely — their flames
bending toward him as if drawn by an unseen wind.

Then, just as he passed the Hall of Shadows, he heard it.

"Lunaris…"

He froze. The voice wasn't in his mind — it came from behind
the door. He pushed it open.

The hall was empty. Only the great banners hung there —
black silk embroidered with the sigil of the crescent moon. But
for a moment, one of them rippled.
And in the ripple, he saw a pair of eyes. Watching. Waiting.

He whispered, "Malrec…"

The torches went out.

Chapter LXV — The Gathering Dusk

The whispers did not stop.
Even when Lunaris left the Hall of Shadows and returned to his dorm, their echo clung to him — not as sound, but as presence. Like a heartbeat he couldn't quite shake.

Ashael, ever alert, prowled the corners of the room, silver eyes flashing each time the lantern flickered.
The wolf's growl was low, uneasy — the kind that signaled danger the human ear could not yet sense.

"Something's watching," Lunaris murmured.

The wolf's gaze snapped toward the window.
Outside, Everveil's towers were bathed in mist, and the moon hung swollen and strange. For a heartbeat, he thought he saw movement within the fog — silhouettes circling the spires, as though shadows had begun to walk the air itself.

An Uneasy Council

By morning, the rumors had spread.
Students whispered of nightmares, of mirrors fogging on their own, of reflections that didn't match their movements.
When the Ebon Vow gathered at their usual table, they found the rest of the Great Hall quieter than ever.

Veyr spoke first. "You all feel it too, right? The Veil's bleeding through again."

Corvus leaned forward, voice low. "Malrec."

Nyx's fingers tightened around the obsidian pendant she wore. "He's only a name in prophecy. He shouldn't *exist* yet."

Lunaris shook his head. "Prophecies don't wait. They unfold."

At that, silence fell between them. Even Ashael, resting at his side, had gone still — his ears twitching toward sounds none of them could hear.

Then came the voice of Headmistress Veyra from the dais above.
"Students," she announced, "the Veil has stirred once more. The northern ridges of Duskwood report signs of breach — a rift pulsing near the ruins of Old Everveil. The Veilguard has requested assistance from the advanced students."

Her eyes found Lunaris's group, lingering for a heartbeat too long.
"The council will choose who is sent."

The words were careful, measured — but the meaning beneath them was not lost. Everyone in the hall turned toward the Vow.

Corvus smirked faintly. "Well, looks like the shadows are calling again."

The Veilguard Envoy

That night, as the others slept, Lunaris stood on the parapet overlooking the northern valley.
From here, he could see the faint shimmer — like a wound in the air, miles away, glowing pale and wrong.

Behind him, boots clicked against the stone.

"You shouldn't be out here."
The voice belonged to Captain Dael Varrow, commander of

the Veilguard detachment stationed at the Institute — a scarred man with eyes like steel and patience like ice.

Lunaris didn't turn. "You saw it too."

"Aye. And I've seen what happens when it grows." The captain came to stand beside him, his black cloak rippling. "It starts as a tear. Then it widens. Then something comes through."

"What's on the other side?"

Varrow's jaw tightened. "Something that remembers *you.*"

He handed Lunaris a folded parchment.
"Orders. The Council's sending your team north at first light. You'll travel with two of my people. This isn't a training mission anymore, boy. Whatever's coming — it's hunting for you."

Lunaris unfolded the parchment and read the seal at the bottom — the insignia of the Everveil Council and the Veilguard intertwined.
He looked up at the misty horizon. "Then we hunt it first."

The Farewell Before Dawn

Before dawn, the courtyard glowed with torchlight as the Ebon Vow prepared their gear.
Veyr secured the packs, Nyx tightened the straps on her bow, and Corvus inspected his twin blades, the moonlight catching on their edges.

"You ready for this?" Corvus asked quietly.

Lunaris adjusted the cloak clasped at his throat, marked with the Umbra crescent. "We don't have a choice."

Ashael padded to his side, fur silvered by the pale dawn light. The wolf's gaze lifted toward the northern sky — toward the rift that pulsed faintly like a heartbeat in the clouds.

The moment felt heavy. Final.

Nyx broke the silence. "Whatever's up there… we finish it. Together."

Veyr smirked faintly. "That's what the Vow's for, right?"

Lunaris met their eyes — each one of them, bound now by more than oaths.
"Then we do what we were meant to do."

The torches flared, the Veil's whisper rolled across the valley like thunder — and the Ebon Vow rode into the gathering dusk.

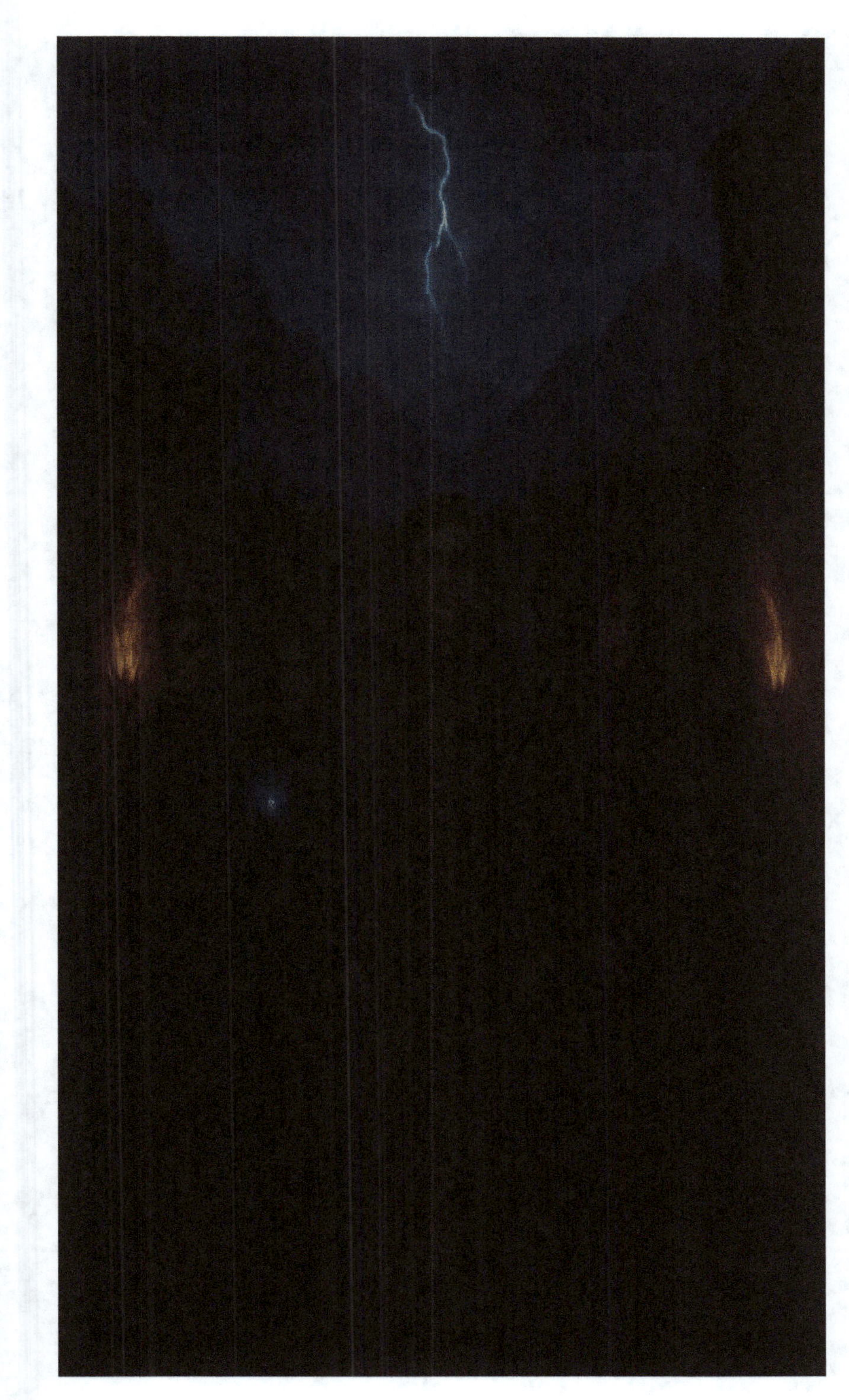

Chapter LXVI — The Northern Veil

The journey north began beneath a sky that refused to
brighten.
Even when dawn should have burned away the mists, the light
lingered dull and gray, as though the sun itself feared to rise
over the mountains.

The four shadows rode in silence — Lunaris in front, Ashael
pacing beside his mount like a spectral guardian, his paws
stirring faint trails of mist. Behind him, Corvus kept watch on
the treeline while Nyx and Veyr whispered to each other over
the rhythmic thrum of hooves.

By midday, the trees grew thin, and the mountains began to
loom — black ridges etched with veins of faint blue light.

The Ruins of Old Everveil

When they reached the old northern path, the first signs of
corruption showed.
The forest had withered. Branches curled like blackened bone.
The snow along the path shimmered faintly, as though laced
with starlight — or ash.

"Veil residue," Veyr muttered, kneeling beside the frost. "It's
eating the world."

Nyx looked ahead, her eyes narrowing. "Then we're close."

They crested the ridge and saw it — the ruins of Old Everveil,
the first academy, long abandoned after the Veil collapsed
centuries ago. Its towers lay half-buried in ice, but one spire
still stood, cracked open like a rib cage.

And above it — the rift.
A wound in the sky, pulsing like a heartbeat. The air around it
shimmered, distorting the clouds into spirals.

The Voice in the Wind

As they approached, the wind began to whisper.
At first it sounded like the sigh of the mountains — but then
the whispers became words.

"Lunaris…"

He froze. The others looked at him.

"You heard that?" Corvus asked.

Lunaris didn't answer. His breath clouded the air, every exhale
visible, though the others' weren't. The world around him had
dimmed, as if shadow itself leaned closer.

The voice came again — softer this time, yet deeper, older.

"Umbra's blood carries the key… and the wound calls for its
heir."

The air cracked with cold. Ashael's fur bristled, his teeth
bared.

"Lunaris!" Nyx's voice snapped him out of it. "You're
freezing."

He blinked — and the world rushed back. The light returned,
and the whispers faded into the distance.

"I'm fine," he lied.

But they all knew he wasn't.

The Breach

When night fell, they set camp in the hollow of a ruined hall. The sound of the rift pulsing overhead never stopped — a slow, rhythmic hum that echoed through their bones.

Veyr, ever the scholar, set up wards along the perimeter. Corvus sharpened his blades in silence. Nyx tended to a small fire, the glow catching in her silver hair.

Lunaris sat apart, his back against a fallen column. Ashael lay beside him, eyes fixed on the sky.

"Something's alive in there," Lunaris whispered.

Nyx looked up. "The rift?"

He nodded. "It's watching. Learning."

"Then we make sure it learns to fear us," Corvus said, standing. His shadow stretched long against the wall — longer than it should have.

They all noticed it, and for a moment, no one spoke.

Then came the sound — a deep, guttural roar rolling down from the mountains.
The ground trembled. The rift flared.

Lunaris rose, drawing his blade — the dark steel of the relic pulsing faintly with his heartbeat.

"Positions," he ordered quietly.

Four shadows turned toward the northern ridge. Snow fell in silence — until the night split open and something vast emerged from the fog.

It wasn't just a creature.
It was a *fragment of the Veil itself*, wearing the shape of a beast — eyes burning like dying stars, wings of mist and shadow.

The First Clash

The fight was chaos and beauty.
Nyx's arrows burst into trails of light as they struck the beast's wings, tearing away plumes of living smoke. Veyr's daggers spun in circles of dark energy, carving sigils midair. Corvus charged headlong, blades flashing silver.

Lunaris called on the shadows — not to hide, but to *command*. They rose from the ground like smoke and wrapped around his sword, and when he struck, the blow echoed with something older than magic.

Ashael leapt, his form flickering between matter and mist, biting into the beast's throat with a snarl that shook the ruins.

The monster screamed — a sound like tearing stone.
It reared back, wings blotting out the moon, before collapsing into a cloud of darkness that spiraled upward into the rift.

When the dust cleared, the night was silent again — but the rift still pulsed, brighter than before.

The Mark of the Rift

As Lunaris approached the spot where the creature fell, something glowed faintly in the snow.
A fragment — like a shard of glass, pulsing with black-blue light. He reached for it.

The moment his fingers brushed it, the mark on his wrist — the one tied to Ashael — flared. Pain seared through his arm.

He fell to one knee, gasping. The shard melted into his skin, vanishing beneath it.

"Lunaris!" Nyx ran to his side. "What happened?"

He looked up, eyes now faintly reflecting the same eerie light as the rift.

"It's not done with us," he whispered. "This was just its messenger."

Chapter LXVII — The Rift's Echo

The wind that followed the battle felt wrong — too still, too *listening*.
Frost clung to the ruins like a veil, and every step they took echoed through the hollow halls of Old Everveil.

Lunaris led the group deeper into what remained of the ancient structure, his sword dimly aglow, its shadow-fire humming against his pulse. Ashael padded beside him, head low, sniffing the air with quiet, restrained tension.

"Something's watching," Veyr murmured.

Nyx nodded. "Not something. *Everything.*"

The Chamber Below

They found the entrance at dawn — a cracked stairway leading beneath the foundations of the ruined spire. The stone was marked with runes long faded, but the Veil residue pulsed faintly between the cracks like veins of dim starlight.

The descent was long. Cold air pressed down as they moved, and by the time they reached the bottom, their breath had begun to form mist.

At the center of the underground chamber stood a shattered obsidian mirror, half-buried in frost.

"The Mirror of Malrec," Veyr whispered. "It's real."

Corvus glanced at him sharply. "You *knew* about this?"

"I read of it. In the archives. It was sealed before the first fall of Everveil."

Lunaris stepped forward, eyes fixed on the mirror's surface. He saw nothing — and yet something within it shifted, almost like it breathed.

The Voice in the Glass

Then came the whisper — clearer now, unmistakable.

"Umbra's blood endures… as the gate was meant."

The mirror rippled like water, and for a heartbeat, Lunaris saw a figure — a shadowed silhouette of a man, tall, regal, crowned in darkness. His eyes burned with blue fire.

"You open the way with every battle, child of twilight. When the moon bleeds, I will return."

The voice fractured into echoes, and the mirror shattered. A wave of cold shot outward, knocking the four of them to the ground.

Ashael leapt forward, placing himself between Lunaris and the shards, his growl deep enough to shake dust from the ceiling.

When the light faded, Lunaris rose — blood running from a small cut on his palm where a shard had sliced him. The wound pulsed faintly with the same dark-blue glow as the rift's light.

The Aftermath

Nyx approached him carefully. "Lunaris… what did it say?"

He didn't answer at first. His reflection in the frost looked older, wearier — like something behind his eyes had seen too much.

"It called me *the gate*," he finally said.

Silence hung heavy. Corvus's expression hardened. "Then we close it before it opens."

Veyr knelt beside the shattered remains of the mirror. "Or it closes *us*. This was a warning, not a prophecy."

Ashael brushed against Lunaris's leg, a low rumble echoing in his chest — half growl, half reassurance.

The four stood together in the dim light of the ruined chamber, their shadows merging into one.

Above, through the cracked ceiling, the rift pulsed once — faintly, like the beat of a distant heart.

Chapter LXVIII — Ashes of the First Gate

The mirror's destruction left the cavern in silence. Only the faint hum of the Veil remained — a low, vibrating tone that sank into the bones and refused to fade.

Lunaris pressed a hand to his side, still feeling the echo of the cold that had lashed through him when Malrec's image appeared. The wound on his palm had sealed, but the faint luminescent mark pulsed beneath the skin like a heartbeat.

Nyx's voice broke the quiet. "That wasn't just a warning."

Veyr crouched by the largest shard, studying the glowing runes carved along its edge. "No. It was a *signal*. When the mirror broke, something beyond it woke up."

Corvus ran a hand through his hair, frustration simmering beneath his calm exterior. "We should've left it untouched."

Lunaris looked toward the remains of the mirror — and in the reflection of one curved shard, he swore he saw it again: a faint, distant flame in the dark, spreading slowly outward, as if from another world.

The Veil Trembles

When they emerged from the chamber, dawn had not yet reached the surface. The rift overhead had dimmed, but veins of blue still laced the clouds like cracks in the sky.

The ground trembled once — faint, but long enough to silence them all.

Veyr glanced toward Lunaris. "That wasn't natural."

"No," Lunaris murmured. "It's the Veil shifting. The mirror was one of the seals."

Nyx turned sharply. "Then what happens when the other seals fall?"

Lunaris didn't answer — but Ashael growled low, his fur bristling as frost flaked off his paws.

In the distance, a deep rumble rolled through the mountains.

Something had *stirred*.

The Night Camp

By the time they reached the ridge overlooking the frozen valley, exhaustion pressed on them all. They built a small fire, its light flickering weakly against the wind.

Corvus unrolled a map, tracing a path toward the nearest Waygate. "We return to Everveil and report to the Council. Whatever this was, they'll want proof."

Nyx nodded, pulling her cloak tighter. "And what if they already know?"

That question hung between them, heavier than the cold.

Lunaris sat slightly apart, the firelight catching on the faint glimmer of the mark in his palm. Ashael rested beside him, muzzle on his knee, eyes reflecting silver in the dark.

"The voice said *I am the gate*," Lunaris murmured, staring into the flames. "What if… it's not metaphor?"

Veyr looked up. "Then we're not guarding the Veil," he said quietly. "We're guarding *you*."

No one spoke after that.

Above them, the aurora shimmered faintly — but within its light, threads of darkness pulsed like veins of ink through glass.

Chapter LXIX — The Gathering Storm

The wind howled through the peaks as the Ebon Vow made their way down the mountain trail. Snow whirled in blinding sheets, biting at their cloaks and stinging their faces. The storm had come fast—unnaturally fast.

Ashael trotted ahead of Lunaris, his paws silent on the frozen ground. The wolf's fur shimmered faintly, his silver eyes cutting through the blizzard like lanterns. He paused, ears twitching, then let out a low, uneasy growl.

"Something's following us," Corvus said quietly, hand tightening on his dagger.

Nyx nocked an arrow without a word, her breath misting in the dark. "How close?"

Before anyone could answer, the snow behind them shifted—something massive moved beneath it. A rumble followed, like a growl from the earth itself.

"Run," Lunaris ordered.

The Beast in the Storm

They broke into a sprint as the ground behind them exploded in a shower of frost and rock. A monstrous shape rose from the snow—a creature born of shadow and ice, with antlers like frozen branches and eyes that burned with Veillight.

It roared, shaking the mountainside.

"Veilspawn!" Veyr shouted, raising his twin daggers. "It followed the rift!"

Lunaris turned, his sword flaring with blue fire as Ashael lunged beside him. The wolf struck first, his fangs sinking into the creature's shadowed leg, tearing through its half-real form. Corvus circled wide, his blade flashing as Nyx's arrows found their mark, each one glowing faintly with runic light.

But the beast didn't fall—it only grew angrier.

Its claws tore through the snow and struck Lunaris, sending him sprawling. His blade flew from his hand and embedded itself in the ground. Ashael howled, his body dissolving into mist to reform beside Lunaris, standing guard as the creature bore down on them.

Veyr shouted over the storm, "We can't kill it here—it's feeding off the Veil!"

"Then we drain it!" Lunaris growled, seizing his sword. "On me!"

The Binding of the Beast

The four of them moved as one. Corvus's sigils ignited, weaving silver chains of shadow that bound the creature's limbs. Nyx fired arrow after arrow, pinning its movements, while Veyr darted between its legs with twin daggers glowing blue-white.

Lunaris stepped forward, his eyes glowing faintly with the same hue as his wolf's. "Ashael," he whispered.

The wolf leapt, merging with his shadow as Lunaris thrust his blade forward. The mark on his palm blazed—the sword struck true, plunging through the creature's chest in a burst of cold fire.

The beast screamed—a sound like shattering glass—and then imploded into mist.

When the silence returned, all that remained was a faint shimmer of Veillight on the snow.

The Storm Breaks

They stood together, breathless, the snowstorm dying as suddenly as it had begun.

Nyx lowered her bow, voice barely a whisper. "That thing wasn't just drawn here… it *knew* where we were."

Corvus wiped frost from his hair. "Which means something's watching through the rift."

Veyr crouched beside the spot where the creature fell, his daggers still glowing faintly. "Then this isn't over," he said. "That was just a scout."

Lunaris looked toward the horizon. The sky had begun to clear, revealing the faint shimmer of the rift in the distance— like a wound that refused to heal.

Ashael stood beside him, fur stirring in the fading wind.

"Then we'd better get stronger," Lunaris said quietly.

The others nodded. And together, the four of them began the descent—toward Everveil, and the storm that awaited them there.

Chapter LXX — Echoes of the Rift

The snow had stopped falling.
The mountain was eerily silent, blanketed in pale frost and the faint shimmer of residual Veil energy. The Ebon Vow trudged through the stillness, the crunch of their boots on the ice echoing against the distant peaks.

Lunaris kept one hand on Ashael's back. The wolf's fur was dimly luminous now, threaded with veins of light where the creature's essence had burned through him during the fight. It pulsed faintly with each heartbeat, as if marking a connection neither had asked for nor yet understood.

"Does it still hurt?" Nyx asked quietly, her voice muffled by her hood.

Lunaris shook his head. "Not exactly. It feels… alive."

Veyr adjusted the straps of his cloak, glancing toward the horizon. "Whatever that thing was, it wasn't acting alone. That wasn't just some creature that slipped through a tear—it *was sent.*"

Corvus was silent for a while, tracing sigils into the frost with his gloved finger. "If the rift is active again, then someone—or something—is stirring it."

Return to Everveil

By the time they reached the academy gates, the sun had begun to set. Everveil loomed in the dusk like a fortress carved from memory and shadow. Silver lamps lined the pathways, their flames wavering in the cold breeze.

They entered through the main archway, the echo of their steps filling the vaulted corridors. Students moved past them, whispering about the recent storms, the strange lights seen over the northern peaks, and the sudden summons to the Great Hall.

"Looks like word's already spread," Nyx murmured.

Veyr gave a short nod. "Let's just hope we're not walking into another trial."

The Headmistress's Warning

Inside the Great Hall, banners of the seven Houses hung heavy in the flickering light. Headmistress Veyra stood before the central dais, her robes dark as the void beyond the Veil. Her gaze swept the room, landing briefly on the four of them before she spoke.

"Something ancient has stirred," she said, her voice carrying easily through the hall. "A surge within the Veil—unnatural, deliberate. The northern outpost was attacked two nights ago by entities of shadow and frost. The rift over the Vale Peaks has widened."

A murmur rippled through the gathered students.

Veyra's eyes narrowed slightly. "The Ebon Vow has already faced one of these entities and survived. Their report confirms the Veilspawn's presence in our world."

Dozens of eyes turned toward them. Lunaris felt the weight of every gaze, but he didn't look away. He could feel the pulse of Ashael's energy thrumming in his veins, faint but insistent— like an echo of the beast's dying roar.

"Everveil will not remain idle," the Headmistress continued. "Each House will contribute to a new watch—one that will act as our first line of defense against the Veil's intrusion."

Her gaze lingered on Lunaris. "The Ebon Vow will lead the first expedition."

Echoes Beneath the Surface

Later that night, the four of them gathered in the House of Darkness common hall. The firelight flickered off obsidian walls, and their relics lay on the table between them—silent, waiting.

Corvus leaned forward. "If this rift's growing on its own, we need to know why. And if it isn't…"

Nyx finished for him softly, "Then someone's trying to open it."

Veyr's hand tightened around one of his daggers. "We need to be ready."

Lunaris looked down at his sword, tracing the runes along its blade. They pulsed once in response—alive, aware.

"The Veil's changing," he said quietly. "And I think it's starting with us."

Ashael lifted his head beside him, eyes reflecting the flame's blue light.
Somewhere deep within the academy, the walls hummed faintly with power—as if the Veil itself had heard him

Chapter LXXI — Shadows at Dusk

The train station at Lake Crescent glowed beneath the waning
evening light. Lanterns burned low, their flames shimmering
faintly against the mist curling from the water. The air smelled
of rain, iron, and the faint whisper of magic that always
lingered near Everveil's borders.

The year had come to an end.
Finals were finished, the halls emptied, and the ancient towers
of Everveil stood silent — watching as its chosen few
prepared to leave.

Lunaris stood with his hand resting lightly on Ashael's back.
The silver-eyed wolf sat beside him, tail still and posture
proud, though his gaze shifted often to the horizon where the
Veil shimmered faintly beyond the forested ridges.

Veyr, Corvus, and Nyx gathered near the edge of the platform,
their cloaks billowing softly in the wind. None of them spoke
for a while. They didn't need to. The silence was heavy with
all they had endured — the battles, the blood, the secrets
carved into their souls.

A Moment of Stillness

Corvus broke the quiet first.
"So that's it. First year down."
He tried for a grin, but it came out tired.

Nyx rolled her eyes and elbowed him gently. "You make it
sound like we didn't nearly die half a dozen times."

"That's exactly why I'm celebrating," he replied dryly.

Veyr leaned against one of the station's pillars, arms crossed, the light catching the silver edges of his twin daggers where they hung at his side. "We got through it. That's what matters."

Lunaris looked at each of them in turn — the faces that had become more than allies, more than friends. The ones the Veil itself had chosen to stand beside him.
"It's not the end," he said quietly. "It's just the pause before the next fight."

Ashael gave a soft, low growl, as if in agreement. The sound drew small smiles from the others. Even Nyx laughed under her breath.

The Shadow Messengers

Veyr reached into his satchel and pulled out four small, black crystal rings, each etched with the sigil of their vow — the crescent encircled by flame.
"Shadow messengers," he explained, handing them out. "Each one bound to the others. Speak your message into it, and the rest of us will hear it. No distance too far — as long as the Veil still listens."

Lunaris turned his over in his hand. The stone felt cool, pulsing faintly with familiar energy.
"Remind me to thank you when it doesn't whisper my private thoughts at three in the morning."

Veyr smirked. "No promises."

Promises in the Dark

The first train whistle echoed across the valley. Nyx turned toward the sound, her hair catching the last of the light. "Guess that's mine," she said softly. "Southbound — toward Valeith Reach."

Lunaris nodded. "We'll meet again before next term."

"Count on it," she said, slipping her ring on before climbing the steps into the train car. She gave one last look through the window, a faint smile ghosting her lips as the train hissed to life.

Veyr was next. "North," he said simply, clasping Lunaris's forearm. "Try not to pick any fights with Veilspawn over the summer."

"No promises," Lunaris replied.

When the second train departed, the platform felt emptier. Only Corvus remained, leaning on a crate, eyes glinting with the kind of exhaustion only earned by surviving what they had.

He glanced over. "See you next term, Umb—" He stopped himself and smirked. "Lunaris."

"Take care of yourself, Corvus."

The older boy nodded once, then vanished into the departing fog.

A Quiet Departure

Lunaris stood for a long time after the final train disappeared, the air thick with mist and memory. Ashael nudged his hand gently, the wolf's eyes catching the dim lanternlight.

"We'll see them soon," Lunaris murmured.
He looked up at the crest above the station arch — the sigil of Everveil glowing faintly against the stone — and felt that strange pull again. The call of the shadows. The promise of what was coming.

Beyond the lake, lightning flickered faintly over the horizon — a silent omen.

The Veil whispered in his mind, words he didn't fully understand but somehow already knew:

"The vow endures."

He touched the crescent mark on his wrist, the faint shimmer of his shadow tattoo visible beneath the sleeve. Then, with Ashael at his side, he stepped into the waiting train.

The doors closed with a soft hiss.
And as the engine rumbled to life, a single echo lingered in the dark — the faint hum of shadow and light intertwined

Epilogue — Echoes Beneath the Veil

Summer took Everveil the way shadow takes a candle—slowly, gently, and all at once.

By dawn the courtyards were emptying. Portals hummed like beehives opening to distant towns; waygates bloomed and folded as students stepped through and dissolved into light. Banners of the Seven Houses hung still as sleep, and the stone that had thundered with training, laughter, and war meetings remembered only footfalls fading toward home.

On the eastern parapet, four figures stood where the wind always found them.

Lunaris rested his palms on the dark stone, gazing across the Cascades. The mark on his forearm—the crescent circled by the wolf's bite—glowed faint as if it, too, were listening to the mountains breathe. He said nothing at first. He didn't need to. The quiet between the four had learned their language.

Veyr adjusted the satchel at his side, serpent ring winking in the light. "Our courier paths are set," he said, voice low. "Shadow messengers will run the coast and the inland routes both. If anything stirs—"

"It already has," Nyx murmured. Wind teased hair from her hood; the faint sheen of the new sigils along her throat caught the morning. "The Veil doesn't close after tasting blood. It remembers."

Corvus huffed a thin laugh. "So do we."

He lifted his hand. One by one they clasped wrists: crescent to raven, fang to coil, song to storm. The old vow—newer than breath, older than fear—carried heat through skin and bone.

"We keep watch," Lunaris said, finally breaking the silence. "We stay ready. And we come when called—no matter how far."

"Even if we aren't the ones being called," Nyx added.

"Especially then," Veyr said.

They broke apart as the bells tolled once, twice. Farewells were not dramatic; they were practical, as soldiers' promises often are. Nyx descended toward the northern spur where a boat waited to carry her downriver through the Duskwood. Veyr turned for the mountain road and vanished piece by piece into mist. Corvus lingered a heartbeat longer, the corner of his mouth quirking with that lopsided defiance that had become a comfort.

"Try not to tame the moon while I'm gone," he said.

"Try not to raise the dead for fun," Lunaris returned.

Corvus's grin widened a fraction. "Who said anything about fun?"

He disappeared into the stairwell. The echo of his boots fell away like a finished spell.

Lunaris stayed until the light turned thin and colorless and the towers cast long spears over the cliffs. When he finally took the western bridge, he glanced once across the campus—the ring where they had been Chosen, the hall where truth had been forced from him like breath in winter, the doors to the Vaults that seemed to watch with half-lidded eyes.

He felt the Veil turn, ever so slightly, the way a sleeper turns toward a sound.

"Soon," he whispered, not as a promise or a fear, but as a fact the world would eventually learn.

He stepped through the gate and was gone.

Far north, where the ridgelines met the ocean in broken teeth, a ruin remembered its name.

Wind moaned through arrow slits black as sockets. The fortress had fallen once—stones peeled like scabs, towers carved open to the marrow—but a shadow can rebuild what a hammer cannot. Inside the shattered keep, frost mapped sigils across the floor, thawing and refreezing in a slow pulse. Something had bled here. Something had been burned out. And yet—

A candle flared in a room that had not held a flame in months.

Not a candle. An eye.

The glow turned, gathering itself along the bones of a man who was not yet living and refused to be dead. Ash drifted up from the floor and threaded into sinew; whispers wound into cartilage; the memory of a heartbeat found its way back to a cage of ribs.

Malrec inhaled.

It was not breath. It was hunger.

He stood with a crack of ice and dust, surveying the wreckage of his old design. The Veil above him rippled like hot air over iron. It would tear clean, he knew. In time. In the right hands.

"Moonborn," he said softly, tasting the word as if it were a fruit not yet ripe. "Little wolf."

He lifted one hand. The air slit open the width of a blade. On the other side, a field of night rolled in slow waves—figures moving beneath the surface like leviathans under black water. They turned toward the gap, attentive.

"Not yet," Malrec said, and the seam stitched itself closed with a faint sound like a string being plucked.

He looked to the south, to the mountain that wore a school like a crown, and smiled with the patience of old winter. "Grow stronger," he whispered to the distance. "I prefer worthy prey."

Snow began to fall inside the room, the flakes the color of ash. He held out his palm and let one settle on the line of his life. It did not melt.

"Soon," he agreed with the boy who could not hear him.

On the road below Everveil, a lone figure walked between firs heavy with new green. Lunaris's pack rode his shoulder; Ashael padded at his side, a shadow that breathed. Where their steps fell, the fog parted as if it recognized a boundary.

A raven called once in the distance. Another answered. He glanced up and the trees were only trees again.

The path rounded a bend and the valley opened—the thin line of a river, the small scatter of farms, a smoke thread from a hearth he knew before he saw the roof. Home wore the hour like a halo. He touched the pendant at his throat, and for a heartbeat it felt warm, as if the memory inside it were awake and listening.

"Almost there," he told the wolf.

Ashael's ears flicked; the tail brushed his calf. The two of them descended the last switchback as evening drew its first veil over the fields.

Above them, so high no human eye could claim it as proof, the sky creased. Only for a moment, thin as breath on glass. A light pressed through and then receded, like a hand testing a door it knew it could open whenever it wished.

Everveil's wards shivered and stilled.

The river kept its song. The farmhouse window lit. Somewhere, far away, a man made of ash began to walk.

And the world, not yet aware of its own intake of breath, held it

Acknowledgments

To the dreamers who walk the edge of shadow — this book exists because you do.

To those who believed in *The Shadow Heir* when it was still only whispers and sketches in the dark — your faith carried light into every page.

To my family, whose patience and love have always anchored me, even when my mind wandered into other worlds.
To my friends and readers — your excitement gave breath to the Veil, your curiosity gave life to its Houses.

To the storytellers and worldbuilders before me, who taught that darkness is not the absence of light, but the space where truth waits to be seen.

And finally, to you — the reader.
For walking these halls, for following Lunaris and the Ebon Vow into the unknown, for daring to listen when the shadows spoke.

Veritas in Umbra, Fortitudo in Tenebris.
Truth in Shadow. Strength in Darkness.

— Stephen M. Ovak
The House of Shadows
Carson City, Nevada

The Everveil Codex

Appendix: Chronicles of the Chosen, Year One of the Ebon Vow

I. The Seven Houses of Everveil

House	Sigil	Domain & Virtue	Motto
House of Shadows	Crescent moon eclipsed by a wolf's head	Shadow, balance, truth	*In shadow, truth endures.*
House of Flame	Phoenix rising through smoke	Fire, transformation, will	*Through destruction, renewal.*
House of Stone	Mountain split by a silver vein	Earth, endurance, strength	*We bend; we do not break.*
House of Tides	Wave curling into a spiral over a single eye	Water, emotion, depth	*All things return.*
House of Storms	Lightning coiled within a ring of mist	Air, motion, power	*Power answers motion.*

House	Sigil	Domain & Virtue	Motto
House of Light	Radiant sun encircled by broken chains	Illumination, purity, freedom	*Truth banishes the shadow.*
House of Mind	Silver eye framed by three runic lines	Awareness, perception, will	*Discipline is the first magic.*

II. The Ebon Vow — Founding Members

Codename	True Name	House	Familiar	Date of Birth	Mark & Relic
Lunaris	Stephen Umbra	House of Shadows	*Ashael —* a silver-eyed wolf of living mist and moonlight	July 17	Wolf sigil on forearm; *Umbra Blade*, a longsword etched with *Veritas in Umbra.*
Corvus	Kael Thane	House of Shadows	*Noctra —* a spectral raven with ink-black feathers and ember eyes	October 31	Raven mark across shoulder; *Necrostaff* of whispering shadowbone.
Nyx	Arienna Valeith	House of Flame	*Cael —* a drake of molten	April 12	Phoenix sigil along spine;

Codename	True Name	House	Familiar	Date of Birth	Mark & Relic
			glass and emberlight		*Obsidian Bow* of mirrored flame.
Veyr	Soren Corren	House of Storms	*Ryn* — a dusk-gray wolf with ember-red eyes	February 9	Twin lightning tattoos on forearms; *Dusk Daggers* forged of stormglass.

III. The Prophecy of the Ebon Vow

"When the moon bleeds twice and the Veil forgets its keepers,
The heirs of shadow will rise as one.
Seven will stand where light and night divide,
Bound by vow, marked by flame,
To seal the gate or shatter it forever."

Known as *The Lunaris Prophecy*, this foretelling was inscribed upon the Altar of the Relics in the Umbra Cavern. It predicts the formation of the Ebon Vow and the coming Veil Reawakening tied to Lunaris's eighteenth birthday.

IV. The Known Relics of the Veil

Relic Name	Bearer	Description
Umbra Blade	Lunaris	Longsword forged of light-drinking steel, merges with its wielder's dagger. Symbol of leadership and the first bond.
Necrostaff	Corvus	Dark staff carved from shadowbone, murmurs lost languages, capable of calling the Veil's echoing dead.
Obsidian Bow	Nyx	Bow of molten shadowglass, string of emberlight. Every arrow ignites mid-flight.
Dusk Daggers	Veyr	Twin blades born of stormglass, hum when danger nears, capable of striking faster than thought.
Vessel Knuckles	Unclaimed	Metal knuckle guards that hum faintly, inscribed with runes of anchoring.
Wraithstaff	Unclaimed	Staff forged of ghost iron and black quartz, rumored to bend shadow constructs.
Lash of Tenebris	Unclaimed	Metallic whips braided with living shadow, their marks never fade.

V. Chronological Record — Year One

Date	Event
July 17	Lunaris's fifteenth birthday — Receives the Umbra family book and begins his initiation.
September 2	Arrival at Everveil Institute — Sorting Ceremony and induction into House of Shadows.
October 31	Corvus's birthday; Lunaris and Corvus become allies.
November 20	Discovery of the Hidden Cavern and first Relic Room; The Ebon Vow is born.
December 20 – January 5	Winter break; Lunaris receives heirloom gifts from his parents.
January 10	Winter term begins; whispers of Malrec's return.
March 4	The "Embers Beneath the Ice" mission — first large-scale Veil confrontation.
April 7	Training intensifies; Veil rifts multiply.
May 25	Finals week; the Ebon Vow returns to Everveil for closing assembly.
May 30	Summer begins; The Ebon Vow disperses for break.

VI. The Umbra Clan Legacy

Motto: *Veritas in Umbra, Fortitudo in Tenebris.*
(*Truth in Shadow. Strength in Darkness.*)

Crest: A wolf and eagle flanking a crescent moon, banner below reading *UMBRA*.
Represents both the **Umbra Clan** and the **Umbra Family**, now considered one and the same. The crest hangs above the family hearth in the Umbra home.

Ancestral Founder: *Erebus Umbra*, the First Walker Between Shadows, patron ancestor of the Umbra bloodline.

VII. The Veilguard and the Outer Academies

Though Everveil stands as the foremost shadow academy in the Pacific Northwest, it is part of a greater network of gifted schools across the United States, each tied to one element of the Veil:

Academy Name	Location	Specialty
Pyrelight Academy	Sedona, Arizona	Fire and Transmutation
Tidefall Academy	Bar Harbor, Maine	Water and Emotion
Stoneward Institute	Boulder, Colorado	Earth and Endurance
Stormrise Academy	Chicago, Illinois	Air and Kinetic Control
Lumenhold Conservatory	Savannah, Georgia	Light and Restoration

Academy Name	Location	Specialty
Mindspire Academy	Boston, Massachusetts	Mind and Awareness
Veilguard Training Corps	Denver, Colorado (Primary HQ)	Powerless and Gifted Defense Agents

The **Veilguard**, drawn from both the powerless and gifted, protects humanity from Veil breaches, serving as the mortal shield when the unseen wars spill into the world of light.

VIII. Known Prophecies and Omens

- *"The second moon shall bleed where winter meets flame."* — recorded by Headmistress Veyra of Everveil, Year One, Spring Term.
- *"When the wolf's shadow drinks fire, the balance will tilt."* — fragment found in the Tenebric Archive.
- *"The forgotten eighth shall awaken."* — author unknown; believed to reference a hidden House or a lost Vow member.

The Everveil Chronological Tracker

Year One — The Shadow Heir

Compiled from the archives of the House of Shadows and verified by the Everveil Council.

Summer — The Awakening of the Heir

July 17 — *Lunaris's Fifteenth Birthday*

- Stephen Umbra (Lunaris) receives the Umbra family tome from his parents, Cael and Elara.
- The Veil stirs for the first time in his presence, marking the start of his awakening.
- Ashael manifests faintly in reflection — the first sign of a destined familiar.

August 2–25 — *Preparation and Departure*

- Lunaris is formally introduced to the history of the Umbra lineage.
- Receives guidance about Everveil Institute and its legacy of Shadows.
- Farewell from Cael and Elara before his journey north to Washington State.

Autumn Term — Arrival at Everveil

September 2 — *Arrival & Sorting Ceremony*

- The Sorting Ring awakens; shadows rise from the stone to judge the new initiates.
- Lunaris is chosen by the House of Shadows.
- Corvus (Kael Thane) introduced as his upper-year mentor; their bond begins.

September 10–30 — *Orientation and Training*

- Lunaris begins classes in Umbral Theory, Veil History, and Shadow Manipulation.
- Early friendship with Kael deepens; hints of the Veil's instability emerge.

October 31 — *Corvus's Birthday / Hall of Lanterns Feast*

- Everveil celebrates the Festival of Shadows.
- Kael shares his story and the burden of the Thane line.
- Lunaris learns of faint disturbances near the mountain's edge — the first sign of Malrec's reawakening.

Winter Term — Whispers in the Veil

November 20 — *The Hidden Cavern Discovered*

- Lunaris, Corvus, Nyx, and Veyr stumble upon the sealed Umbra Cavern.
- The ancient Relic Room awakens, choosing them as the first four of the Ebon Vow.
- Each receives their Relic and Mark; the prophecy of the Shadow Heir is revealed.

December 1–15 — *The First Missions*

- Minor veil rifts begin opening across the Pacific Northwest.
- The group trains in secret, learning to control their relics and familiars.
- Ashael fully manifests — a silver-eyed wolf of the Veil.

December 20 – January 5 — *Winter Break*

- Lunaris returns home to the Umbra estate.
- Receives heirloom gifts from his parents — a Veil pendant and a runic signet.
- The Umbra Clan Crest is officially hung above the family hearth.

Spring Term — The Veil Awakens

January 10 — *Classes Resume / Winter Term Opens*

- The Everveil Council addresses growing Veil disturbances.
- Malrec's name begins surfacing in restricted archives.

February 9 — *Veyr's Birthday*

- Small celebration within House of Shadows dormitories.
- Group dynamics deepen — subtle hint of Nyx and Veyr's closeness.

March 4 — *Mission: "Embers Beneath the Ice"*

- The Vow faces its first major Veil creature.
- Massive ice-bound wraith defeated; Ashael absorbs its essence, granting Lunaris shadow-flame control.

- Their victory earns attention from the Everveil
  Council.

April 7–20 — *Advanced Training & Bond Strengthening*

- The Ebon Vow continues missions under supervision.
- Veil corruption grows stronger; students begin
  reporting nightmares.
- Nyx and Veyr's bond solidifies.

April 12 — *Nyx's Birthday*

- Quietly celebrated within the House of Flame common
  hall.

Late Spring — The Fracturing Balance

May 1–10 — *Mission: "Whispers Through Frost and Flame"*

- Second major mission leads to confrontation with
  hybrid Veil entities.
- Lunaris's relic evolves, merging completely with his
  dagger.
- The group's unity tested — but their vow holds.

May 20–25 — *Final Examinations*

- All Houses converge for final assessments.
- Ebon Vow's actions remain classified but whispered
  about through the halls.

May 30 — *End of Year Gathering / Farewell Feast*

- Closing assembly at Everveil Hall.
- The Vow promises to stay connected via shadow messengers.
- Each member departs for summer, returning to their families or training grounds.

Summer — The Quiet Between Storms

June 5–August 31 — *Interlude of Shadows*

- Lunaris trains privately with Cael Umbra.
- Corvus joins a Veilguard scouting mission in the south.
- Nyx and Veyr begin corresponding through encoded shadow letters.
- Unseen, Malrec begins to move once more.

Key Annotations: Year One Summary

- **Number of Active Vow Members:** 4
- **Known Relics Claimed:** 4 / 7
- **Known Familiars Manifested:** 4
- **Veil Rifts Recorded:** 12 confirmed across the Northwest territories
- **Everveil Headmistress:** Veyra Lorne
- **Year-End Classification:** *Stabilized; Threat Level Amber*

Excerpt from the Archives of the House of Shadows:

"The first year marked the awakening of the Shadow Heir and the binding of the Four.
The Veil quivers, waiting. The next eclipse draws near."
— *Everveil Chronicle, Vol. I, Closing Entry*

From the Shadows of the Past...

Book II of the Everveil Chronicles

The Veilborn Ascendant

The Veil stirs once more.

The Vow has been scattered — each bound to their own path, each marked by the choices they made beneath the mountain.

In the quiet stretch of summer, new shadows awaken. Old enemies take shape. And far beyond the walls of Everveil, the name **Malrec** begins to whisper across the riftlines like a storm waiting for dawn.

As Lunaris trains beneath the silver light of the Umbra Crest, his bond with Ashael deepens… and with it, the truth of what he truly is.

Nyx's flames begin to devour her dreams.
Veyr's daggers sing louder each night.
Corvus walks among the Veilguard, where duty and darkness collide.

The world beyond Everveil grows restless — Veilstorms spread, relics awaken, and an unseen power calls from the depths of the forgotten eighth House.

And when the **moon bleeds twice**, the true Shadow Heir must choose: to guard the Veil…
or to open it.

By Stephen M. Ovak

The House of Shadows — *Carson City, Nevada*

"The night remembers those who dare to walk it twice."